In Deep Water . . .

"By mistake?" I repeated. "You think someone tracked down the water valve and took a wrench to it by *mistake*?"

"You'd be surprised," Owen said, laughing. "This isn't the first time an overeager volunteer did something they shouldn't have and didn't want to admit it."

I didn't say anything more. I mean, the guy had a lot more experience at construction work than I did. Still, I didn't feel nearly as sure as Owen that the valve had been opened accidentally.

"Uh-oh. I know that look." George raised an eyebrow at me. "What are you thinking, Nancy?"

NANCY DREW
girl detective™

Available from Aladdin Paperbacks

NANCY DREW

DREW

girl detective ™

#23

Troubled Waters

CAROLYN KEENE

Aladdin Paperbacks
New York   London   Toronto   Sydney

This book is a work of fiction. Any references to historical events, real people, or real locales are used fictitiously. Other names, characters, places, and incidents are the product of the author's imagination, and any resemblance to actual events or locales or persons, living or dead, is entirely coincidental.

❦ALADDIN PAPERBACKS
An imprint of Simon & Schuster Children's Publishing Division
1230 Avenue of the Americas, New York, NY 10020
Copyright © 2007 by Simon & Schuster, Inc.
All rights reserved, including the right of
reproduction in whole or in part in any form.
NANCY DREW is a registered trademark of Simon & Schuster, Inc.
ALADDIN PAPERBACKS, NANCY DREW: GIRL DETECTIVE, and
colophon are trademarks of Simon & Schuster, Inc.
Manufactured in the United States of America
First Aladdin Paperbacks edition April 2007
10 9 8 7 6
Library of Congress Control Number 2006924387
ISBN-13: 978-1-4169-2513-2
ISBN-10: 1-4169-2513-9

Contents

Troubled Waters

After the Flood

"Voila! Two dozen turkey sandwiches with lettuce, cheese, and tomato, all wrapped and ready to go," I said.

I held up a tray in the middle of our kitchen and grinned at my two best friends, Bess Marvin and George Fayne. The three of us had been making sandwiches for the past hour—maybe longer. We were totally surrounded by cold cuts, lettuce, bread, cucumbers, sliced peppers . . . you name it.

"I've got ham on whole wheat," George added. She tore some plastic wrap from a roll, stretched it around the sandwich she'd just made, and added it to a pile on the counter.

"And I'm almost done with these veggie wraps," George's cousin Bess spoke up, standing at the counter next to George. "They look delicious, if I say so myself."

"Hey, no tasting," George teased. "Remember what Cathy said. People over at the Historical Society and the Senior Center are waiting for these sandwiches."

I'll be the first to admit that my friends and I can get food obsessed. Give us three spoons and a pint of ice cream, and we're in heaven. But this time we'd actually been motivated by something other than our bottomless-pit stomachs.

We'd had record-breaking spring rains in our area. When you live near a river, like we do, wet weather can cause big trouble. Our town of River Heights hadn't been hit too badly. The cliffs along the river kept water from overflowing. But some of the low-lying towns south of us hadn't been so lucky. Every night we heard on the news how the floods were the worst our area had seen in a century. Hundreds of people had lost their homes. They were being put up temporarily in places like the Historical Society building, the Senior Center, local hotels—anyplace that had room . . . including the guest room and the sofa bed in the Drew family home. My house, in other words.

Bess, George, and I turned as the kitchen door opened. Our housekeeper, Hannah Gruen, came in.

Her niece, Cathy Fogler, was behind her, along with Cathy's seventeen-year-old son, Brad. They carried bulky cardboard boxes, which they angled through the doorway. It didn't take a detective to see that the three of them were related. They all had the same blue eyes and broad cheeks. But Hannah and Cathy were round and curvy and on the short side, while Brad had the tall, muscular build of an athlete. He towered over the rest of us as he placed his boxes on the counter near George.

"Where should we put these sandwiches, Hannah?" George asked.

Hannah has lived with Dad and me ever since my mother died, when I was three. The kitchen is usually her territory. But in the two weeks since Cathy and Brad had been staying with us, Cathy had done even more cooking than Hannah. So I wasn't surprised when Cathy was the one who answered George's question. Dropping her boxes on the floor, she took a look around.

"Brad, why don't you help the girls load sandwiches in these boxes? Aunt Hannah and I will pack up the cakes and quiches we made this morning," Cathy said. She nodded at a dozen quiches and chocolate cakes that covered the kitchen table. "I'm sure everyone will appreciate a tasty meal after all they've been through."

3

"You make it sound like the floods have only been hard for other people. You and Brad lost your house too," Bess said, bending to place veggie wraps in one of the boxes. "*And* your business."

I saw a sad gleam in Cathy's eyes. "It figures the floods would hit right *after* I redid the kitchen so I could handle more catering jobs. I never imagined the whole house would collapse like it did. Brad and I didn't take anything but some clothes when we left," she said. "Now it's all gone. Brad's baby pictures . . . everything."

I wasn't sure what to say. But then Cathy smiled and said, "We're just lucky to know people like you and your dad, Nancy. I don't know where Brad and I would be if you hadn't insisted that we stay here. And Mrs. Mahoney has me delivering meals to flood victims all over the county. I'm actually busier now than I was before the floods."

Mrs. Mahoney is like a one-person good-deeds factory in River Heights. She runs the Mahoney Foundation, which has contributed to just about every worthy cause around. Half the buildings in town have her name on them. Making sure flood victims had enough to eat was exactly the kind of thing she would do. And by hiring Cathy to supply meals, Mrs. Mahoney was helping to keep Cathy's catering business—called the Catered Table—going strong too.

"The floods have been hard on Brad, though," Cathy went on. She sighed as Brad headed out the kitchen door with a box that George had just finished packing. "Our whole neighborhood in Cedar Plains was pretty much destroyed. About half of the boys on Brad's basketball team are staying with friends or relatives. It'll be months before they can get back in their homes—if their houses are still standing."

"Ouch," George said, grimacing.

Cathy nodded. "Thank goodness the school gym didn't flood, that's all I can say. Basketball is the one normal thing a lot of the kids have left," she said. "That's why their coach is holding practice this week, even though school's closed for vacation."

I felt an ache in the pit of my stomach. It was the same ache I got every time I saw another story on the news about a building that had been washed away or a family pet that was missing. So many people had lost so much. I wished I could do more to help.

Maybe it was a coincidence that Dad called right then. He likes to check in with me when he's at the office, especially when I'm trying to solve a mystery and he's worried I might be in some kind of trouble. Not that there was any mystery in my life at the moment. Still, Dad's timing was perfect. As soon as I heard what he had to say, the ache in my stomach turned into an excited buzz.

"Guess what?" I said, dropping the phone on the counter. "Dad just told me that—"

"Tell us while we drive to the Historical Society," Cathy cut in. She headed for the door with a box of quiches. "We were supposed to be there ten minutes ago!"

"Let me get this straight. We're going to be part of the Helping Homes renovation team?" George said twenty minutes later. "Those guys do *amazing* work."

"That's for sure. Did you see the TV special about that old factory in California? Helping Homes made it over into apartments for people with disabilities," Bess added. "They had six teams of volunteers working like crazy. The whole place was ready in less than a month."

We had just arrived at the River Heights Historical Society—though, to be honest, it looked more like a shelter than anything else. Cots and bags of people's personal belongings filled the open room where lectures and exhibits were usually held. The two long tables in the adjoining library had been cleared of old books and maps and letters. I counted about two dozen people who sat there ready to eat the lunch we'd brought—from little kids to a wiry, white-haired man who used a walker. Cathy had been right about them appreciating a tasty meal. They all dug in with gusto when we handed out sandwiches and slices of cake.

"Well, now Helping Homes is doing the same thing with the old Davis Foundry," I said, making my way down one of the tables with plastic cups of milk and water.

"That run-down old metalworks next to the river?" Bess said. She handed veggie wraps to two teenage girls while George held the box. "It shut down ages ago."

"In nineteen fifty-six, according to Dad. But he says the building is solid. And it's huge. When Helping Homes is done, there'll be one hundred new apartments for people who lost their houses in the floods."

Cathy grinned over her should at me as she handed out plates of quiche. "Including Brad and me?" she said, shaking her head. "You're sure, Nancy?"

"Definitely. Dad is handling some of the legal details, so he ought to know," I told her. "He knew Bess and George and I would want to help, so he signed all three of us up as volunteers. Actually, tons of people are helping. Dad said the whole Lowell

University basketball team is going to be working with us."

"The Bullets?" George glanced over the top of the bulky box, and her eyes lit up. "They won the state championship, two years running! Their starting forward is awesome. J.C. Valdez. I'm pretty sure he's from around here."

Cathy nodded. "J.C. went to Cedar Plains High," she said. "All the guys on Brad's team idolize him. The way they see it, he's living proof that a local boy *can* make it big."

"Anyway, I guess we'll meet the whole team later," I said. "All the volunteers are supposed to meet at the Davis Foundry at four o'clock for a press conference."

As we moved to the second table, the heavy wooden door to the Historical Society banged open. A teen-age boy with a mop of reddish hair ran in. He looked excitedly around until his gaze landed on Brad.

"Put that stuff down," the boy said, nodding at the tray of cake slices Brad was holding. "We've got to head over to the school right away. Coach wants to talk to the whole team. We're going to be training with the Bullets!"

Brad's eyes snapped toward the other boy. "The Bullets? Cam, are you serious?" I noticed that Brad hadn't kept pace with the rest of us, but was stuck halfway down the first table. He'd been held up by

8

the older man who had snow-white hair and a walker. The guy didn't seem to have heard what Brad's friend Cam had said. He just hung on to Brad's arm and kept on talking.

"Poor Otis is out there all by himself," he said in a worried, raspy voice. "I called and called, but that old dog wouldn't come. The water got so high that I had to leave without him."

Cam glanced impatiently at his watch. "Coach Stanislaus wants us to meet *now*," he said to Brad. "The Bullets are going to be working on some building renovation. Coach wants us to volunteer too. *And* we'll be training with the Bullets every night."

"Awesome!" Brad started to move toward Cam, but the white-haired man had a firm grip on his arm. "Um, I've really got to go, Mr. Fillmore. . . ."

"Looks like Brad needs some backup," George said under her breath.

Putting down my tray of drinks, I walked back to the other table and said, "I'll take over here, Brad. Um, Mr. Fillmore, have you tried calling the animal shelter?"

I felt sorry for Mr. Fillmore. He wasn't exactly fit enough to go looking for his dog, and it had to be awful not knowing what had happened to him. Mr. Fillmore really didn't want Brad to go. Even after I took over handing out the cake, he hung on to Brad's sleeve and kept going on—and on—about Otis. It took Brad about five more minutes before he finally broke free and left with Cam.

"Did you see how happy they looked?" Cathy commented, watching the boys disappear through the door. "Working with the Bullets is a dream come true for those boys."

"For us, too," Bess said as she and George finished handing out sandwiches. "We get to help flood victims *and* hang out with the top basketball players in the state. How great is that?"

We were all so psyched that I didn't think we could stand to wait until the Helping Homes press conference at four o'clock. But Cathy kept us busy. After delivering meals to people at the Historical Society, the Senior Center, *and* the River Heights Inn, we barely had time to change before heading to the old foundry.

"There's the turnoff," Bess said, leaning forward in the backseat of my car. She pointed to our right, and I saw a battered, weathered-looking sign marked DAVIS FOUNDRY. Just beyond, a narrow drive curved out of sight behind the trees.

I turned onto it, and we zigzagged through more trees. The narrow road, edged by a strip of muddy ground, rose uphill toward cliffs that overlooked the river. The woods were so thick around us that we didn't see the old foundry until we came out of the trees right next to it.

"Whoa!" George said, blinking into the sudden daylight. "Talk about massive!"

There, perched at the edge of the cliffs, was a huge, rambling brick building. It looked as if a couple of football fields could fit inside of it. The brick exterior was grimy and worn, but it was clear that work to renovate the old foundry had begun. A blue tarp had been stretched over tent poles outside the building, and plywood and other building materials were piled underneath it. New windows had been put in from top to bottom, and a crew was steam cleaning the brick to reveal a startlingly bright reddish brown beneath the grime.

"There's the RH News truck!" Bess said as I pulled into the parking lot. About thirty cars, trucks, and SUVs were parked there. We pulled to a stop right next to the van from our local TV station, with its satellite dish on the roof. A truck from the local newspaper, the *River Heights Bugle*, was parked a few cars down.

"We're in luck. Even the weather is cooperating," I said.

The sky wasn't exactly blue and cloudless, but I spotted a couple of glaring rays where the sun was trying to peek out from the haze. Not that it was enough to dry out the deep puddles around the foundry. And the rushing waters of the swollen river below reminded us of all the storms we'd had recently. But at least it wasn't raining—for the moment, anyway.

As we walked toward the old foundry, I saw that about fifty or sixty people had gathered on the muddy ground outside the factory's huge double doors. The two news crews hovered around them with their photographer and cameraman. At the center of the crowd was a guy who didn't look much older than Bess and George and me. His brown hair had been spiked and tinted blond at the ends, and he wore a leather tool belt over his jeans and denim shirt.

"That's Owen Jurgensen!" Bess said, grabbing my arm. "He's the one who started Helping Homes. I recognize him from that TV special I saw. See the way he's all over the place, talking to a million people at once? The guy's made a career of multitasking. That's how he gets buildings fixed up so fast."

Owen Jurgensen did seem to be everywhere. In the short time it took us to walk over to the group of volunteers, he posed for a picture with Mrs. Mahoney, talked to some guys delivering supplies, and handed out green Helping Homes work hats to volunteers.

"Isn't that Luther Eldridge?" I said, peering at the middle-aged man who had just approached Owen Jurgensen. Luther runs the River Heights Historical

Society, and he knows everything about the history of our area. He was holding what looked like a couple of framed photographs, but I couldn't tell for sure. My view was partly blocked by a bunch of tall guys wearing matching yellow team jackets.

"It looks like the Bullets are here too," George said, her eyes focused on the guys in the jackets. "Check out the one with the ponytail. I'm pretty sure that's—"

"J.C. Valdez!" a voice spoke up behind us.

I turned to find Brad walking with his friend Cam. They both wore royal blue Cedar Plains team jackets. Behind them other guys from their team were getting out of cars and heading toward the foundry in groups of three and four.

"The Bullets' star forward?" I said. Looking back at the guys in the yellow jackets, I saw that one of them had a ponytail dangling out from his Helping Homes hat. He spoke to the two reporters while the cameraman and photographer caught him on film.

"J.C. is the main reason the Bullets won the state championship this year," Brad told us. "Everyone says he's going pro at the end of the year. He's the one who arranged to have the Bullets train us this week."

"Your mom told us J.C. used to play on the Cedar Plains team. I guess he wanted to give back to the team where he got his start," Bess said.

"Pretty cool, huh?" Brad raked a hand through his blond hair, his eyes shining with excitement. "You know, Cam's brother used to play with J.C. And now Cam and I are co-captains, just like J.C. and Craig used to be."

Brad was talking a mile a minute, but Cam just kept walking toward the foundry with his hands in his pockets. It struck me as kind of odd. I mean, I would have expected Cam to be more enthusiastic. But I didn't have time to ask questions. Bess grabbed my arm and pulled me toward the group.

"Come on! Everyone's lining up for the photo," she said.

The scene around us was pretty chaotic. Volunteers were running from the parking lot, the guys who were cleaning the bricks were making a racket with their pressurized hoses, a truckload of beams and Sheetrock was being unloaded, and everyone was talking at once.

I had to jump to the side to keep out of the way of two men carrying plywood. As they headed toward the tarp where the supplies were, they angled behind J.C. Valdez and the reporters.

"When I heard about the floods, I knew I had to do something. After all, Cedar Plains is my hometown. My own parents had to evacuate the house that's been in Mom's family since the eighteen hundreds,"

J.C. was saying. "I found a new place for them over in Woodburn, but I know plenty of people weren't so lucky. If the Bullets' work with Helping Homes brings attention and money to flood victims, I feel we've done our part. . . ."

As Bess, George, and I squeezed in among the crowd, I spotted another guy delivering building materials. He had thick reddish brown hair and a T-shirt with REYNOLDS BUILDING SUPPLY printed on it. He barreled toward us from the parking lot with two long wooden beams balanced on his shoulder. He didn't seem to notice that the tips of the beams were just a few feet from J.C. Valdez's back.

"Watch where you're going!" I called.

The guy was totally oblivious. "Coming through!" he shouted.

He turned, and the beams on his shoulder swung in an arc—straight toward J.C. Valdez.

2

Rivals

Horrified gasps rose up around us.

"J.C., look out!" shouted one of the guys on the Lowell team.

Not that J.C. had time to move out of the way. The beams flew toward his head.

At the last second the guy from Reynolds Building Supply shifted and the beams dipped lower. They smacked into the backs of J.C.'s legs, sending him flying.

"Hey!" he cried. A painful grimace twisted his face as he hit the muddy ground. Then a wall of yellow team jackets closed in around him.

"Think he's okay?" George asked, biting her lip.

We didn't have to wait long to find out. J.C. burst through the knot of teammates a moment later. Mud covered one side of his pants and jacket, and his face was burning red. He stormed over to the guy who had hit him with the beams.

"What's the big idea?" J.C. demanded.

The guy took his time setting the beams down next to the other supplies under the blue tarp. "It was an accident," he mumbled. But when he finally straightened up, he didn't seem apologetic. Far from it. A satisfied smirk stretched from ear to ear.

J.C. blinked and peered closely into the other man's face. "Craig? Craig Reynolds? *You* did that?" he said.

Apparently, these two knew each other. But I didn't get the feeling they were best buddies. J.C. shoved his palms against Craig's chest. "You knocked me down on purpose! Don't you know you could have hurt me?"

"Hey, *you're* the expert on hurting people," the guy named Craig shot back. "We both know who would be the star of the Lowell team if you hadn't tripped me up in the regional finals."

"What's going on?" George whispered.

I didn't have a clue. But Brad leaned close to us and said in a low voice, "That's Cam's brother, Craig Reynolds."

"The guy who was co-captain with J.C. in high school?" George asked.

Brad nodded. "Craig injured his knee in the

regional finals one year. The doctors tried surgery, but they couldn't repair the damage," he explained. "Craig never played basketball again."

"But Craig made it sound like J.C. hurt him," I said. "Like it wasn't an accident at all."

"Craig and J.C. had some kind of collision on the court," Brad explained. "Everyone figured it was just a freak accident that Craig's knee was hurt so bad. But Cam told me Craig is totally convinced that J.C. tripped him on purpose."

"That's a serious accusation," George said. "Why would J.C. injure his own teammate?"

"Money," said Brad. "Lowell hands out sports scholarships, but only to a few top players."

"So . . . ," Bess said, scraping the toe of her work boot across the muddy ground, "Craig thinks J.C. hurt him on purpose to make sure *he* got the Lowell scholarship?"

"Yup. Meanwhile, any chance Craig had of playing college ball was wrecked," Brad finished. "After high school he went to work for his dad's building supply company. He helps Coach Stanislaus with our team, but that's not exactly as exciting as a pro sports career."

"No wonder he's so bitter," I said. "It must have hurt to see his dreams go up in smoke—while J.C. went on to become one of the hottest players in college basketball."

"Yeah, but that doesn't make it okay for Craig to go after J.C. with those beams. Anyway, just 'cause Craig *thinks* J.C. hurt him on purpose doesn't mean he really did," George said. She glanced toward the front of the crowd, where the shouting match between Craig and J.C. was growing louder.

"You don't *really* care about people who lost their homes," Craig said, jabbing a finger at J.C. "The only one you care about is yourself! Joining up with Helping Homes is just a big publicity stunt to you. Nothing like getting your name in the paper to make the pro teams notice you, eh?"

"Oh, they notice me," J.C. said. "I've been the top player at Lowell for two years running. I've got what it takes to make it in the big leagues, which is more than anyone ever said about you. . . ."

Craig looked so angry, we could practically see the steam coming out of his ears. "Someday people will realize what a big fake you are," he told J.C. "Everything you do will turn out to be a big flop!"

People around us were shifting uncomfortably. Not that I blamed them. Hearing J.C. and Craig fling insults back and forth made me feel squeamish too—especially when I saw that the news cameras were catching the whole thing.

"Leave it to the press to cover a juicy fight instead of the renovation," I said, rolling my eyes.

I was glad when Owen Jurgensen stepped between J.C. and Craig. "Calm down, you two. I'm sure we can work this out," Owen said smoothly.

I guess managing so many volunteers had made him an expert at dealing with tricky situations. I don't know how he did it, but within seconds, Craig and J.C. were shaking hands. The next thing we knew, Craig was heading back toward his truck, and the reporters were lining the rest of us up for the publicity photo in front of the entrance to the Davis Foundry. Owen was all smiles, chatting with volunteers, helping to organize the crowd, and getting Luther Eldridge to tell reporters about some framed photographs of the old foundry that he'd brought from the Historical Society. By the time we all said "Cheese!" everyone seemed to have totally forgotten about the argument.

"Thanks, everyone! I'll see you all here tomorrow morning at seven sharp," Owen said as the crowd broke up. He chuckled at the chorus of groans that rose from the volunteers. "I know it's early, but the sooner we renovate these apartments, the sooner one hundred families who lost their homes in the floods will have a new place to live."

"Including Brad and Cathy," Bess said, grinning.

Brad and Cam had been right next to us during the press conference, but now I saw that they and the rest of their team had gathered around an older man I guessed was their coach. Brad's face was filled with anticipation as Coach Stanislaus led the team over to J.C. Valdez and the rest of the Lowell players.

At least, he *tried* to approach J.C—but a petite, dark-haired girl had glued herself to J.C.'s side and was fawning all over him.

"Oh brother," George muttered, flicking a thumb at the girl. "When did DeeDee get here?"

George, Bess, and I have known Deirdre Shannon since we were kids, but we're not exactly friends. The truth is, we're about as compatible as fire and water. Deirdre never misses a chance to look down her nose at us, so we usually keep as far away from her as we can.

"You were *amazing* in the state championship game, J.C.," Deirdre gushed, hanging on to his arm. "I was there, of course. Daddy got tickets right at center court. . . ."

"Why is she here, anyway? Don't tell me she's going to risk ruining her manicure in order to volunteer with Helping Homes," Bess murmured.

"She must be," I reasoned. "Why else would she be at the foundry?"

"Um, Mr. Valdez?" Brad's coach spoke up. But there wasn't much of a chance that J.C. could respond since Deirdre had pulled J.C. around so his back was to everyone but her.

"I'd be happy to show you around River Heights, J.C.," Deirdre offered. "After all, you can't spend *all* your time in this dreary place."

"Is she for real?" asked someone next to me. I turned to see a young woman about my age wearing overalls, a paisley blouse, and a well-worn tool belt with the name TANYA stamped into the leather. She had chocolate brown skin, braids that were pulled back in a ponytail, and dark eyes that stared at Deirdre in disbelief.

"Thinking about other people isn't usually a big priority for Deirdre," I told her.

"Then someone should change her priorities," the girl said. As she strode over to Deirdre, I saw a determined gleam in her eyes. "Excuse me," the girl said. "If working on the foundry is so *dreary*, then why did you volunteer?"

"Volunteer?" Deirdre's tone implied that working with Helping Homes was about as high on her wish list as being sentenced to a chain gang. "Don't be ridiculous. I only came here to invite J.C. and the rest of the Bullets to a party I'm having in their honor."

"And to make sure she gets her picture taken with J.C. Valdez," Bess added under her breath to George and me.

Sure enough, Deirdre turned toward the reporters with a wide smile, leaning close to J.C. "It'll be day after tomorrow, at seven p.m. All the best people will be there."

"Oh brother," George mumbled. "Can't someone shut her up?"

"Actually, maybe someone can," I whispered. I nodded toward the girl with the paisley blouse and tool belt. She continued to face Deirdre, and this time the gleam in her eyes was definitely mischievous.

"Well, if the *best* people will be there," she said, "then the *entire* Helping Homes renovation crew is invited, right?"

"Everyone?" Deirdre's smile faded. "I, uh . . ."

"That's a great idea," Coach Stanislaus piped in. "I guess we can skip one night of practice for a party."

George chuckled and grinned at Bess and me. "Let's see DeeDee try to weasel out of inviting us," she whispered.

But Deirdre couldn't—not with the *River Heights Bugle* and RH News cameras pointed at her.

"Well, um . . . yes, of course," she said at last, flashing the fakest smile I've ever seen.

"Congratulations," George said as the girl with the tool belt and braids came back over to us a minute later. "I think you just knocked us off the top of Deirdre Shannon's most-hated list."

"I'll take that as a compliment," the young woman said. "I'm Tanya Deschanes, by the way."

"I'm Bess, and this is Nancy and George," Bess told her. Nodding at the tool belt Tanya wore, she asked, "Do you work on the Helping Homes staff?"

"I guess I look the part," she said, laughing. "I'm actually studying to be a veterinarian, but I'm pretty comfortable with a hammer and wrench. My dad has a thing about buying old houses and fixing them up. I've helped him since I was a kid."

"Well, the personalized tool belt is a great touch," Bess replied. "I wouldn't mind getting one myself."

Most people would never guess that petite, blond-haired Bess is actually a fix-it whiz. Tanya smiled at her and said, "Listen, I was talking to some of the other volunteers before about going out to dinner. We're going to be spending a lot of time together on the renovation, so we figured we might as well get to know each other. Want to join us?"

One look at Bess and George, and I knew our answer. "We'd love to," I agreed.

"Great! A couple of the Bullets are coming too," Tanya told us. "We just have to wait until they're done with the press."

Deirdre left, and Brad's teammates finally had their chance to meet the Bullets. The two teams stood together posing for the RH News and the *Bugle*. Brad and Cam, the two co-captains, stood right up front next to J.C. Valdez. Brad looked as if he couldn't stop grinning, but Cam didn't seem nearly as excited. He kept glancing moodily toward the parking lot.

"Look who's still here," I murmured, frowning.

Craig Reynolds was leaning against the cab of the Reynolds Building Supply truck. His arms were crossed over his chest, and his steely gaze was fixed on J.C. Valdez.

3

Troubled Start

I woke up the next morning with the uneasy feeling that something wasn't right. Maybe the problem was just that it wasn't even six o'clock yet. I mean, getting up before it's even light out could make *anyone* feel unsettled. And it didn't help that I kept remembering the sullen, angry way Craig Reynolds had stared at J.C. Valdez from the parking lot of the Davis Foundry.

Don't make such a big deal of it, I told myself as I got dressed, went into the kitchen, made myself some coffee, and had a seat. Volunteering with Helping Homes will still be great.

After all, George and Bess and I had had a fantastic time with Tanya and the other volunteers the night before. We'd met a couple guys from the Bullets, including a point guard named Travis who'd talked sports with George practically the whole evening. Everyone was really psyched about working with Helping Homes.

"Nancy?"

I looked up from the kitchen table to see Cathy standing in the doorway in her bathrobe. "Have you seen Brad? I just checked the sofa bed in the family room, but he's not there," she said. She crossed to the kitchen door and peered through the window. "His car's gone."

"Maybe he headed over to the foundry early?" I suggested.

"Maybe." Frowning, Cathy poured a cup of coffee and sat down next to me. "To tell you the truth, I haven't seen or spoken to him since he left the Historical Society yesterday. He usually calls to check in, but . . ."

"Yesterday he didn't?" I guessed.

Cathy sighed. "I fell asleep after midnight, and he wasn't home yet. And now he's up and gone so early. The only reason I know he was here at all is that the sofa bed is rumpled. He obviously slept in it."

"He was excited about training with the Bullets," I said. "Maybe he couldn't wait to—"

I broke off as two quick blasts of a car horn sounded outside.

"Oops! That's George. Gotta go." I gulped down the last of my coffee, grabbed my work hat, and jumped to my feet. "I'll tell you what. When we get to the foundry, we'll tell Brad to call and check in with you, okay?"

"Thanks, Nancy," Cathy said with a smile. "I'm probably worrying over nothing."

I ran outside and climbed in the backseat of George's car. She and Bess were both dressed for the job, right down to their work boots and green Helping Homes caps. Bess turned to grin at me from the passenger seat. "Ready to burn some calories and get some calluses?" she asked. "Something tells me building these apartments is going to be a serious workout."

"No pain no gain," George quipped, turning in the driver's seat. "Anyway, it's for a good cause. Where's Brad?"

"That's what Cathy wants to know too. He probably left early for the foundry," I said.

When we got to the Davis Foundry, volunteers were stumbling sleepily toward the sprawling brick building. I didn't see Brad—though if he'd gotten there early, he was probably inside already. Following the crowd, we headed through the massive double doors at the entrance.

"Wow!" Bess said. "Is this place cool or what?"

We hadn't actually come into the foundry during

the press conference the day before. Now that we did, all I could do at first was stare. The room we were standing in was cavernous—at least three stories high with some second-floor brick offices or workrooms overlooking the wide-open space. At least, the *original* room of the foundry was wide open. But Helping Homes was already starting to transform it. Only the area near the double doors had been left open. I figured that would be the lobby. An old clock over the door, with DAVIS FOUNDRY etched into its metal frame, had been left untouched. But the space beyond was filling up with a skeletal frame of wooden and aluminum beams where new walls would be. A new second floor had already been built, with a new balcony that jutted up against the bricks of the old offices, and a metal staircase that zigzagged up to it. I could see where the elevators would be installed and a framework of wooden beams outlining the ground-floor hallways to the left and right of us. Winding through the beams was a network of shiny new pipes and electrical wires.

"Good morning, all!" Owen said, speaking though a megaphone a few feet away from us. He stood next to some rolling racks filled with more saws, hammers, drills, wrenches, and safety goggles than I'd ever seen in one place. "We're going to start off with a tour, so grab some coffee and doughnuts."

I'd been so busy checking out the construction

that I hadn't noticed the table next to the entrance, with a coffee urn and doughnuts on it.

"Check it out," George said. She leaned over the table to gaze at some framed photographs hanging on the wall above it. "These must be the photos Mr. Eldridge brought from the Historical Society yesterday."

"Right you are," Owen said, coming over to us. "They're just copies, of course. The originals are over at the Historical Society." He pointed at the closest photograph, of welders working on slabs of metal next to a glowing furnace, with sparks flying everywhere. "That one was taken right where we are now, as a matter of fact."

A second photo showed a machine that churned out a roll of flat metal three times as big as the man who operated the machine. There were two others as well, plus a framed floor plan of the old foundry, but Owen didn't give us time to look at them closely.

"Okay, everyone. We've got a lot to get done today, so let's start our tour," Owen said, speaking through the megaphone once more. He smiled as Tanya hurried through the doorway with her tool belt in her hands. "Latecomers can join us as they get here."

Tanya dropped her tool belt near the coffee table, next to backpacks and jackets that other volunteers had piled there. She caught up with Bess and

George and me as we followed Owen farther into the foundry.

"Did Owen say what we'll be doing today?" she whispered.

Bess shook her head. "I guess we'll find out after the tour," she said.

Up ahead Owen headed between the beams that framed in a long hallway to the left of the lobby. "As you can see, we've already built an extra floor and have started framing the halls and apartments," he said over his shoulder. "Plumbing and electricity are almost finished. Now we'll be working in teams to do the rest."

"Everything?" one guy asked, shooting a daunted look around.

Owen laughed. "It's not as overwhelming as it sounds," he promised. "We'll work in teams, with a Helping Homes staffer like me in charge of each group. We'll be putting up Sheetrock . . ."

"What's that?" Bess asked.

"The boards that make up the walls," Tanya explained. "They're made of compressed plaster with a coating of paper that makes the walls smooth. There's a stack of them over there."

Tanya pointed to large paper-coated boards that leaned against some beams, alongside rolls of fluffy pink insulation. The slabs of Sheetrock looked pretty big—the boards were about four feet by eight feet and almost an inch thick. I wasn't sure I could lift even one by myself. As I glanced into the maze of beams on either side of the hallway, I saw other materials scattered about: plywood, boxes of nails, more insulation, spare pipes, and wires.

"Teams will also work to insulate walls, install cabinets, floors, bathroom fixtures . . . ," Owen went on. "Of course, we've tried to keep details from the old foundry wherever possible. The clock in the lobby is being fixed, and several old brick ovens are being converted to fireplaces."

"Cool." Bess glanced around, then frowned and said, "Where's Brad? I thought you said he came here early, Nancy."

"Oops, I totally forgot to look for him," I admitted. Scanning the faces around us, I saw that a lot of guys from Brad's team had arrived. I recognized some of the players from the Lowell team, too, but Brad was still missing in action.

"I don't get it. Why isn't he here yet?" I whispered. I circled around some plywood and insulation that had been stacked on the floor. "I mean, he left the house before I even got up. Where else—"

I broke off talking and cocked my head to the side. Sputtering, gurgling noises echoed from the pipes around us.

"What's that?" Bess said. "Sounds like—"

Before she could get another word out, water started spurting from a pipe set against the beams right next to us.

"Hey! What the . . . ?" Bess cried, trying to block the spray with her hands.

We all jumped back, but fountains of water burst from *more* pipes behind us.

"Oh my gosh!" Tanya cried. "The whole foundry is flooding!"

4

Waterlogged!

I ducked behind some beams, wiping water from my face. Shrieks echoed in the cavernous space. Coffee cups dropped as volunteers scattered in all directions.

"The pipes are open where faucets and tubs and sinks haven't been installed yet," Owen stammered. Water streamed across the worried grooves in his forehead. "The water main was turned off, but someone must have opened it!"

"That Sheetrock is getting ruined!" Tanya cried. She sprinted to the panels of plasterboard and started pulling them away from the sprays of water.

Owen was already racing past us on his way back toward the lobby. "Move everything you can while I shut the main valve again!" he called.

George and I grabbed a couple of rolls of insulation.

"Ugh," George said, grimacing at the soggy stuff. It looked like cotton candy that had been left out in the rain. "This looks totally ruined."

Volunteers scrambled all over, moving everything we could away from the spurting pipes. A minute later the water stopped gushing.

"Over here, everyone!" Owen called from the direction of the lobby.

We headed toward the sound of his voice, squeezing water from our hair and clothes. Tanya pinched a corner of soggy Sheetrock from one of the panels she had moved. It squished between her fingers like mud.

"This can't be good," Bess muttered.

Other volunteers seemed to share her concern. I heard a lot of worried murmurs as we worked our way back to the front of the building. I was glad to see that the lobby, at least, was still mostly dry. Water pipes ran along one side of the open area, but not through the center where people had dumped their belongings next to the refreshment table and rolling carts of tools. A handful of late arrivals stood near the table staring at us. Travis, the guy from the Bullets who'd been out with us the night before, took one look at George's wet hair and clothes and asked, "What happened?"

"I can answer that," Owen spoke up. He peered

from around the corner of a doorway set into the bricks. "Come over here, everyone."

He led us into a separate room filled with water heaters, boilers, and fuse boxes. Half a dozen pipes twisted along the wall like branches of a tree, coming together at a larger pipe just above the floor. Water lay pooled on the concrete floor beneath the pipe.

"This is the main water valve," Owen said, touching the pipe. "All it takes is a few turns of a wrench, and the water for the entire building can be turned on and off," he explained. "Obviously, someone turned it on by mistake."

"By mistake?" I repeated. "You think someone tracked down the water valve and took a wrench to it by *mistake*?"

"You'd be surprised," Owen said, laughing. "This isn't the first time an overeager volunteer did something they shouldn't have and didn't want to admit it."

I didn't say anything more. I mean, the guy had a lot more experience at construction work than I did. Still, I didn't feel nearly as sure as Owen that the valve had been opened accidentally.

"Uh-oh. I know that look." George raised an eyebrow at me. "What are you thinking, Nancy?"

I went down a mental list of all the things that nagged at me. "Well, there was that argument yesterday, and now this," I said. "Not to mention that Brad *still* hasn't shown up."

Not that I had a clue as to what those things had to do with one another. I quickly scanned the faces around us, but all I saw were looks of concern. Nothing suspicious. "I don't know . . . maybe nothing weird is going on," I added, shrugging.

As Owen led us all back to the lobby, I saw J.C. Valdez come through the double doors. Owen glanced at him quickly, then checked his watch. "Enough delays. Let's get started," he said briskly. "Volunteers, when I call your name, join your team leader. . . ."

Three men and a woman—all wearing caps labeled HELPING HOMES STAFF—stood to one side. As Owen introduced them, I saw Tanya bend to pick up her tool belt from among the piles of belongings on the floor.

"Hey, where's my wrench?" I heard her say under her breath. She pushed a finger through an empty leather loop next to her hammer. "It was right here."

As Tanya searched among the backpacks and jackets, I gazed distractedly at the orange rubber handle of her hammer. Warning bells went off inside my head. "Be right back," I whispered to Bess and George. "I want to check something."

I put on my work gloves and walked back to the

room with the boilers and water heaters and scanned the maze of new pipes that twisted along the brick walls. "No wrench so far," I murmured.

Lowering my gaze, I walked slowly among the new boilers, water heaters, and electrical boxes.

"Hey . . . what's this?" I said, stopping next to one of the heaters. I nudged something with my toe, and immediately, I heard the scrape of metal on the concrete floor. As I bent down, I spotted the tip of an orange rubber handle.

"Jackpot," I said to myself, holding up Tanya's wrench.

Bess and George were helping Tanya pick through the things in the lobby when I returned. "Hey, where'd you find that?" Tanya asked when I held out the wrench to her.

Volunteers were separating into groups as Owen called their names. Seeing him frown in our direction, I lowered my voice to a whisper. "Someone used it to open the main water valve," I said.

"Well, don't look at me. I was with you guys at the other end of the foundry when the water came on," Tanya said. "Anyway, why would someone take *my* wrench? There are tools all over the place."

"She has a point," Bess said, nodding at the rolling tool carts. "It's almost as if someone wanted people to *think* Tanya did it, when . . ."

Bess's voice trailed off, and she stared at something on the wall above the coffee table. Rather, she stared at an empty space where something was *missing* from the wall.

"What happened to the photos? Weren't there five frames before?" she said. "Now there are only two."

Sure enough, just two framed photographs remained. As I gazed at them, it suddenly hit me. "*That's* why someone opened the water valve," I breathed out.

Bess, Tanya, and George stared at me blankly.

"It was a diversion," I explained. "While we were all getting soaked, whoever opened the valve took the photos."

"But who?" George wondered. Planting her hands on her jeans, she scanned the crowd of volunteers in the lobby. "No one here looks like they'd steal."

Tanya frowned as she slipped her wrench into its spot on her tool belt. "Besides, renovating the foundry will help so many people," she added. "Why would anyone try to wreck what we're doing?"

5

Getting Even

I think I know why," a voice offered.

I hadn't realized anyone was listening to us. But when I turned, I found J.C. Valdez standing at my elbow. Now that he was so close, I realized that J.C. wasn't as tall as I'd thought when I'd seen him talking to reporters and joking with his teammates. He was just half a head taller than I was, but he made up for his lack of height with a quick, agile way of moving. His alert eyes shifted to take in everything around him.

"It's no secret that Craig Reynolds hates me," J.C. told us. "He's always been jealous of my talent on the court. Craig can't handle that pro teams are already recruiting me, while his career went nowhere."

He had a point. Still, I felt myself bristle at J.C.'s arrogant tone. "What does Craig's jealousy have to do with someone stealing old pictures of the foundry?" I asked.

"*And* making sure we start the renovation with a big, soaking-wet disaster," J.C. added. "Didn't you hear Craig yesterday? Shouting about how he hopes everything I do is a big flop?"

Tanya stared at J.C. in total disbelief. "Are you saying you think Craig wants to make sure the foundry renovation fails just because *you're* volunteering?" she asked.

"Sure," he answered. "He'll do anything to make me look bad. I saw his truck when I got here, so I know he's around."

"It's his job to bring building materials here," Bess pointed out. "It doesn't make sense that he would wreck such a worthwhile project when his family is supplying wood and Sheetrock and stuff for us to use."

Her argument didn't seem to convince J.C. He just shrugged and said, "People do crazy things to get revenge."

"I guess turning on the water could be Craig's way of getting back at you, but . . ." I turned to gaze at the spot on the wall where the three missing frames had hung. "Why would he take those photos? They're just copies. We can always get new ones from Mr. Eldridge, so taking them doesn't really hurt the renovation."

"Excuse me! A little attention, please?"

Owen Jurgensen's amplified voice made us turn. That was when I realized that all the volunteers were standing in groups—except for Bess, George, Tanya, J.C., and me.

"We're already getting a slow start, thanks to the accident with the water valve," Owen went on. "You five need to join your teams so we can get to work."

I opened my mouth to say that I was pretty sure the water had been opened on purpose, not by accident. But Owen seemed determined not to hold up the volunteer teams any longer.

"Tanya, Bess, you'll be working on Team A with Marlene," he said, pointing to a young woman who wore a HELPING HOMES STAFF cap over her blond ponytail. "Nancy, George, and J.C., you're on Team C with Wilson."

He waved us over to a brown-haired guy who looked like he was about thirty. He was handing out hammers to all of the other volunteers in our group, Travis and Cam among them. As we walked over to them, Cam's eyes were glued to J.C. He looked embarrassed when J.C. gave him a friendly look.

"You're co-captain of the Cedar Plains team, right?" J.C. said. "What's your name?"

"Cam," Cam told him. "The team is totally psyched that we're going to train with the Bullets this week."

I noticed that he didn't tell J.C. his last name—not that I was surprised. Cam probably didn't want to advertise that his brother was the one who had knocked J.C. down the day before.

"We're going to teach you boys a few moves that'll knock your socks off," J.C. continued, winking at Cam. "You're working with real pros now, not just local has-beens."

"That's, uh, great," Cam mumbled. But I saw the uncomfortable way he stared down at his feet. As J.C. moved over to Travis, Cam turned to me and said, "How come Brad isn't here?"

I scanned the crowd, then sighed. "I was hoping maybe *you* would know," I said.

"Beats me," Cam said, shaking his head. "He was going to give me a ride today, but he called last night to say he had something to do first," Cam said.

"Something to do *before* seven a.m.?" George said, raising an eyebrow.

We didn't have time to talk about it any longer. Owen clapped his hands loudly and said, "Let's get to work, everyone! And remember, the word for today is 'Sheetrock.' We've got one hundred apartments to finish, and they all need walls. That means nailing Sheetrock to the beams, then taping and plastering the seams to make them smooth."

Wilson led our team to an apartment on the newly constructed second floor of the old foundry. Actually, it didn't look like much of an apartment yet. A skeleton of beams marked where the walls would go between the living room, kitchen, bathrooms, and bedrooms. Wilson split our team into smaller groups and gave each one a different room to work on. Once he showed us how to nail planks of Sheetrock over the beams to make the walls, we went to work.

For the next few hours we were too busy to think about Brad—or about who might have opened the water valve and taken the photos of the foundry. George and I lifted and hammered so many sheets of plaster wallboard in place that the muscles in my arms ached. Walls covered more and more of the open beams, and we gradually lost sight of J.C., Cam, Travis, and the other volunteers. The sounds of hammering echoed through the foundry until Wilson announced that it was time to break for lunch.

When we got to the lobby, I saw that the coffee urn had been replaced with dozens of bulging bagged lunches. George took a paper bag and peeked inside.

"Sandwich, chips, an apple. . . . Looks good to me. I'm starved!" she said.

I grabbed a bag for myself, as well as a couple of bottles of water from a case on the floor next to the table. Most of the volunteers were heading outside, so George and I followed.

The day was mild and bright. Except for the still-muddy ground outside the foundry—and the swollen river below the cliffs—there was no sign of the wet weather that had caused so much flooding and destruction.

"There are Bess and Tanya," George said. She stepped around a muddy patch of ground, heading toward the cliffs. Mud gave way to a wide strip of solid rock overlooking the river. Dozens of volunteers sat on the rocks eating their lunches in the bright sunshine. Bess and Tanya sat about ten feet from the edge, using their flattened bags as makeshift plates. They waved us over, but I hesitated when I saw Cam and a bunch of his teammates hovering around the Bullets farther down the rocks.

"I'll catch up with you," I said to George.

Jogging over to Cam, I said, "Can I talk to you for a sec?"

Cam turned a surprised look my way. "Uh, sure. What's up?" he asked, stepping away from the other guys.

"I was just wondering," I began. "Did you help your brother deliver materials to the foundry this morning?"

"Kind of," he told me. "I mean, Craig gave me a ride, but I couldn't help him with the delivery. I was late, so I ran to catch up with everyone."

Cam's gaze shifted to the parking lot, and he added, "Man, it's about time Brad got here."

Squinting into the sunshine, I saw Brad's tall figure getting out of his beat-up old sedan. As he walked toward the foundry, I saw that mud caked the bottoms of his sneakers and dirt smudged his jeans and T-shirt.

"What'd he do, get lost in a swamp?" I muttered.

Brad's gaze flickered our way. But instead of coming over to us, he looked quickly away and headed toward the foundry building.

"Brad!" I called.

Brad kept walking, without turning toward me. He didn't stop until I ran up to him and touched his arm.

"Didn't you hear me?" I asked. "Where were you all morning? We got worried when we didn't see you."

Brad raked a hand through his hair. "I . . . I just had something to do, that's all," he told me.

"Well, give your mom a call, all right?" I said. "I promised her you would."

"Hmm? Okay . . . sure," he said distractedly. He

kept glancing nervously around instead of looking me in the eye. "Oh, there's Mr. Jurgensen. I'd better go talk to him and find out what I should do."

Brad practically ran away, leaving me to stare after him. When I walked back over to the rocks near the cliffs, Bess, George, and Tanya all looked at me expectantly.

"So, where *was* Brad all morning?" George asked.

"I still don't know," I said, sitting down next to them and opening my bagged lunch. "He totally avoided talking to me."

"Weird," Bess commented.

I had to agree with her. "He's been through a lot because of the floods, but this is the first time I've seen him act so ... I don't know ... secretive," I said. I glanced toward the entrance to the foundry, where Brad and Owen were talking, then shook myself. "Anyway, I guess we've got other things to think about."

"Like trying to find out who could have opened the water valve and stolen those photographs?" asked George.

"Exactly," I said.

For the rest of our lunch break George and Bess and I talked to volunteers and Helping Homes staffers. Unfortunately, we didn't learn much. A few people saw Craig stacking Sheetrock and boxes of hardware under the tarp outside the foundry. No one remembered seeing him inside. No one recalled seeing anyone go into the room where the main water valve was either. When we went back inside at the end of the break, I wasn't sure what to think about J.C.'s theory that Craig was trying to get at him by hurting Helping Homes.

"It does seem a little far-fetched," George said. We glanced behind us, where J.C., Travis, Brad, Cam, and Tanya followed in a big group. Brad seemed more relaxed now. He was actually smiling and laughing while he talked with Tanya. "I just hope nothing else happens, that's all."

Inside, Bess joined her team on the first floor, while George and I headed up the metal staircase. We were almost to the second floor when we heard a scream downstairs, followed by an angry outburst.

"Hey! Who wrecked my work?"

George and I both stopped short, and George whipped her head around. "That sounded like Bess!" she said.

The two of us raced back down the stairs, weaving around Cam, Travis, and some other volunteers who were behind us. "I think she's down there," I said, heading for the hallway that led left from the lobby of the foundry.

"There!" George said, as we sprinted down the

hallway. She pointed to the end of the hall, where a crowd spilled out of one of the doorways.

As George and I squeezed inside, I saw an entry hall, living room, and kitchen area similar to those in the apartment where George and I had worked all morning.

"Bess?" George angled around a guy wearing protective goggles—and then stopped short. "Uh-oh," she moaned.

Bess and Tanya stood at the front of the crowd, staring in horror at the living room wall. Panels of Sheetrock had been put up, but the wall looked far from perfect. A ragged hole three feet around had been smashed into it. Chunks of plaster, paper, cement, and smashed bricks covered the floor at their feet.

But what really caught my attention were the three words someone had sprayed on the wall in dripping silver paint:

J.C. GO HOME

A knot twisted in my stomach as I read the message. "I guess J.C. wasn't imagining things when he told us he's a target," I said.

6

J.C. Go Home

W ho would write something so hateful?" Bess asked.

"It's not just hateful. It's destructive," Tanya said angrily. "We just finished nailing up that Sheetrock before lunch. Now we'll have to rip off the wrecked part and do it all over again!"

We all turned as Owen made his way through the crowd. He took one look at the wall and scowled. I could see he was upset, but I guess he didn't want people to panic. "Calm down, everyone," he said, speaking above the anxious murmurs that echoed in the crowded apartment. "Let's get back to work. I'll handle this."

Volunteers began filing out of the apartment, but George and I hung back.

"I don't get it," Owen said, still frowning at the

50

spray-painted message. "Helping Homes renovations have never been targeted this way before."

"Didn't I tell you Craig has it in for me?" We turned to see J.C. Valdez standing in the doorway with his arms crossed over his chest. He stepped aside to let people leave, then nodded at the spray-painted message. "He's messing up the renovation just to get at me."

"Helping Homes is getting hurt a lot more than you are," Owen pointed out. He kicked at the bits of plasterboard and brick. "Every time something like this happens, it costs Helping Homes money and puts us farther behind schedule. We're going to have to repair the bricks, put up new Sheetrock. . . . It's not like we're a big corporation. Every setback costs money we don't have."

I didn't want to make his day even worse, but I figured now was the time to tell Owen about the missing photos—and about finding Tanya's wrench near the water valve. Owen listened quietly, his arms crossed over his chest.

"Jeez. I noticed some of the frames were gone, but we were so busy . . . ," he said. "I figured they'd turn up somewhere." He shook his head, frowning. "You really think someone turned on the water to distract us so they could take the photos?"

"Looks that way," I said, nodding.

"Nancy has lots of experience solving mysteries," Bess added. "We'd already been trying to figure out who took the pictures, and—"

"Hey, look!" I said, stepping over to the ragged hole in the wall. I hadn't looked closely at the damage before, but now as I crouched down, I noticed that the hole went deeper than I'd realized. A lot deeper. "There's a whole room back there!"

"What?" Bess exclaimed. She, George, Owen, Tanya, and J.C. crowded close behind me.

A stale, musty smell hit my nose, and I had to stifle a sneeze. Light from the living room windows filtered through the ragged hole. As I leaned in, I realized that an old doorway had been blocked with cinder blocks. Now that it had been broken through, I saw a dark, dusty room. It wasn't very large, maybe six or eight feet square. All I could make out at first were dusty cobwebs that dangled from the ceiling and a thick coat of dust on the floor. But then Owen shined a flashlight around—and we all gasped.

"What a mess!" Bess exclaimed.

Whoever had busted through the wall hadn't stopped there. Holes had been bashed in the dusty bricks of the hidden room, too. Smashed bricks and cinder blocks lay in piles on the dusty floor.

"Uh-oh," George murmured. She pointed into

the half darkness, and I saw a glint of silver on the wall. Owen shined his flashlight at it, and the beam lit up another spray-painted message.

"'Go back to Lowell,'" Owen read. He gazed soberly over George's shoulder at J.C. "I guess that means you, huh?"

"Guess so." J.C. stared at the message with an unreadable expression on his face. Then he straightened up and stepped away from the wall. "It's pretty clear who wrote it," he said.

"One thing is for sure," I said, sitting back on my heels and gazing up at him. "We need to talk with Craig Reynolds."

"I must have hammered a couple thousand nails today," George said about five hours later.

She and Bess and I were just getting out of her car outside Cedar Plains High School. "My calluses have calluses!" Bess said, holding up her hands. "The muscles in my arms feel like Jell-O from lifting all that Sheetrock."

My muscles ached too, but it was going to be a while longer before I could sink into a hot bath at home. "At least we finished covering the beams with wallboard at the foundry," I said as we headed across the parking lot toward the gym doors. "I think Owen appreciated that some volunteers stayed late—even if we did have to miss the beginning of Brad's practice session with the Bullets."

"Well, we didn't miss all of it, anyway," Bess said. She nodded toward the gym doors in front of us. One door was propped open, and through it we heard clapping and cheers.

"I just hope Craig is here," I said.

"Brad said he helps out with the team, so he probably is," George said, heading through the door. "Actually, it sounds like half of River Heights is here!"

Based on how packed the gym was, you would have thought we were there for an NBA championship game, not a high school team practice. We had to climb high up into the bleachers to find some empty seats. Cheers, hoots, and clapping echoed off the walls, so that we could hardly hear one another.

From what I could tell, the practice part of the evening was over, and now the Bullets were playing on their own. The boys from the Cedar Plains team sat in the first row of bleachers, red-faced and sweaty. They cheered along with the rest of the crowd while the Bullets dribbled and passed the ball on the court.

While the crowd cheered, I scanned the row of Cedar Plains players. "There's Craig," I said, nodding at the end of the row. He was sitting next to Coach Stanislaus, scowling darkly as J.C. stole the ball from another player and sent it sailing through the hoop.

"Yeah, but check out who's *not* there," George commented.

I took a second look at the Cedar Plains players—and then frowned. "Brad," I said. "I don't get it. First he misses half a day of working on the foundry, and now he's missing practice, too."

"He was so excited about training with the Bullets," Bess said. "Why would he skip it?"

"Beats me," I said, shrugging. "He left the foundry at the same time as the rest of the players. If he didn't come here, where *is* he?"

I stared out at the court. I was beginning to think maybe Cathy was right to worry about him. I hadn't been watching the Bullets, but now I saw that J.C. Valdez had the ball. He was a blur as he twisted past one of his teammates, faked a pass, and then landed a high-arching, three-point shot from mid-court.

"No wonder J.C. was named most valuable player of the championship game," George said, shouting above the deafening cheers. "He's awesome!"

J.C. did a little victory dance, then turned to look straight at Craig Reynolds. "Now *that's* talent!" he crowed, smirking.

"Jeez, does he have to rub it in?" Bess said. "I mean, if Craig caused the damage at the foundry, why is J.C. saying things that will get him even madder?"

Craig sat there, as stiff as stone. His cheeks turned an angry red, and he balled his hands into fists at his side. For a moment I was afraid he might jump up and punch J.C. Instead, he just sat there, staring daggers at J.C. until the Bullets stopped playing, a short time later.

"Now's our chance to talk to Craig," I said, getting to my feet. People around us were putting on their jackets and moving down the bleachers toward the doors. By the time we reached the floor, the Bullets were mobbed with fans asking for autographs. At least, *most* of them looked like fans.

"Uh-oh," I said as Craig Reynolds pushed his way up to J.C.

Something told me Craig wasn't going to ask for an autograph. I moved toward the two guys, but not fast enough. "You don't think I've still got talent?" I heard Craig say to J.C. He got right in J.C.'s face and jabbed a finger into his jersey. "Maybe I can't run like I used to, but I can still hit the hoop from the foul line a thousand times better than you."

"Yeah, right," J.C. scoffed. "Care to prove it?"

The next thing we knew, Craig grabbed a ball from the floor and stormed toward the foul line. "You're on!"

I hesitated on the sidelines as the two of them

began taking practice shots. "So much for talking to Craig . . . for a while, anyway," I said.

But as I watched people stream out of the gym to the parking lot, another idea hit me. "Did you guys notice whether there's a Reynolds Building Supply truck outside? Maybe the same truck Craig used this morning to deliver materials to the foundry?"

"I wasn't looking for it when we parked," Bess said. "But it can't hurt to look for it now. If Craig *did* wreck my wall, maybe we'll find a sledgehammer or whatever he used to smash it."

"Or those missing photos," George added.

A minute later the three of us were outside scanning the parking lot. All around us, people were getting in cars and driving toward the parking lot exit. "There!" Bess said, pointing to our left.

Some headlights flashed across my face. When I could see again, I spotted the Reynolds Building Supply truck at the end of the second row of cars. Bess, George, and I hurried toward it.

"I'll keep an eye on the gym doors," Bess offered. She stopped a few feet away from the truck and turned to face the school. "The last thing we need is for Craig to come out and catch us."

While George circled to the back of the truck, I tried the driver's door. "Locked," I muttered.

Pressing my face against the window, I peered inside. Except for a take-out coffee cup and some crumpled fast-food wrappers, I didn't see anything.

"There's a bunch of stuff back here, Nan," George called softly. "Help me look through it."

She was standing on the rear bumper, staring into the open truck bed. Climbing up beside her, I saw a jumble of cardboard boxes and wood half hidden beneath a tarp. "Hmm," I said, pulling the tarp aside.

A couple of sheets of plywood and some beams covered the bottom of the truck bed. Half a dozen boxes sat on top of them. I reached for the two boxes closest to me and opened the cardboard flaps. "Let's see . . . screws, some kind of pipe connectors . . ."

George was opening more boxes next to me. "Washers, doorknobs . . . ," she murmured. There was a pause, and then I heard her draw in her breath. "Nancy, take a look at this!"

George tilted the open box toward me, and I saw three rows of cylindrical silver cans.

"It's spray paint," I realized. "Silver spray paint."

7

Lies and Excuses

T hat's not all," George said. She counted the cans, shifting them to show me an empty spot in the bottom corner. "One's missing."

"So maybe Craig used it to write those hate messages to J.C.?" I said. Pulling the tarp farther aside, I looked beneath it. "There's just more plywood here. No empty can. And I don't see the photos that were taken from the foundry or a sledgehammer."

Bess looked at us expectantly when we rejoined her at the front of the truck. "So?" she asked. Her eyes widened when George and I told her about the spray paint we'd found. "So J.C. was right about Craig!" she said, shaking her head in amazement.

"Looks that way," I said. "Come on. Let's go talk to him. He probably won't be happy that we snooped around in his truck. But we've got to do everything we can to get to the bottom of this. The whole foundry renovation could be at stake."

The gym had pretty much emptied out by the time we returned. Other than a few spectators in the bleachers, the only people left were J.C.'s teammates, Coach Stanislaus, and the boys on the Cedar Plains team. Craig was still taking shots from the foul line, so Bess, George, and I sat in the bleachers behind Cam and the other guys. Cam half frowned when he saw me.

"Where's Brad?" he whispered. "Coach is really steamed at him for skipping practice."

I wasn't thrilled about how Brad was acting either. But at the moment I was more concerned about talking to Craig than tracking down Brad.

"What's the score?" I asked, nodding toward the court.

Cam's eyes flitted toward his brother, and he said, "J.C. sank twenty-seven shots before he missed. Craig made twenty-three so far, and he's still going."

At the foul line Craig bounced the ball twice, then sent it sailing toward the net. It bounced off the backboard, then dropped through the hoop.

"Yes!" Cam said under his breath. "Four more, and he wins. . . ."

Craig was already getting ready for his next shot. His face was a mask of concentration as he bounced the ball twice, then twice again, before shooting it toward the net.

Again the ball hit the rim. But this time, instead of dropping through the hoop, it angled off to the right and missed.

Hoots and cheers erupted from J.C.'s teammates. Hands flew up to give him high fives and clap him around the shoulders. A self-satisfied smile spread across J.C.'s face as he stepped over to Craig and held out his hand.

"Nice try, Craig," J.C. said. "But like I said, you're just not in my league."

Craig swatted J.C.'s hand away. Ignoring J.C. completely, Craig walked over to the bleachers and grabbed his warm-up jacket.

"Come on, Cam," he said, and then headed for the doors.

Craig didn't slow down or turn around. By the time Bess, George, and I caught up to him and Cam, they were already outside.

"Craig?" I called. "Can we talk to you?"

Craig stopped just outside the double doors and turned toward us with a scowl. "Do I know you?" he asked.

"We're part of the Helping Homes volunteer crew working at the Davis Foundry," Bess told him. "We saw you there yesterday."

"And?" he said impatiently.

"There were a few incidents today at the foundry," I began. "Someone's causing damage and putting the renovation behind schedule."

Craig's expression remained stony as we told him about the water, the missing photographs, and the holes that had been smashed in the walls. If he knew about the damage, he showed no sign of it.

"Someone painted hate messages on the walls too," I finished. "Hate messages to J.C. Valdez."

For the first time all night I saw Craig crack a smile. "You mean I'm not the only guy around here who doesn't think J.C. is a superhero? Well, that's . . . Hey, wait a minute." Craig shoved his hands in his pockets and stared at us. "Are you saying you think *I* had something to do with the damage?"

His angry gaze made me gulp, but I held my ground. "The messages were spray painted in silver," I said. "And we found a box of silver spray-paint cans in your truck."

"You found . . ." Craig's scowl deepened, and he took a step toward me. "You've got a lot of nerve, nosing around in my things," he spat out.

"Well, *you've* got no right to wreck the Helping Homes renovation just to get back at J.C. for being more successful than you!" Bess shot back. "Don't you even care about the people who'll get new apart-ments in the foundry?"

"I care plenty about Cedar Plains," he said. "Don't you think I know how lucky my family is that we still have a home, when so many people have lost theirs? Why do you think I'm at the foundry every day with more materials for the renovation? It's because I *do* care!" Craig gave a bitter laugh, shaking his head. "J.C. can come here for a week and make a big splash, but he's just doing it for the publicity. He doesn't care what happens to the people here."

"Well, whoever wrecked that wall today sure hates J.C. And you're the only one we've seen who fits that description," Bess pointed out.

"J.C. must have an enemy you don't know about," Craig insisted, "because I didn't damage anything at the foundry."

Turning away from us, Craig stormed toward his truck. Cam shot an embarrassed glance at Bess, George, and me before following. As we watched them get into Craig's truck, George let out a sigh.

"Talk about bitter," she said.

"And jealous," I added. "But Craig really does seem to care about Cedar Plains and everyone else who's been hurt by the floods. Besides, we can't prove that the paint used to write those messages came from his truck."

At that moment the gym doors opened and J.C. Valdez and the rest of the Bullets came out. They were all laughing and joking around. J.C. tipped an imaginary hat to us as they passed.

"See you tomorrow, ladies," he said.

"Yeah. Thanks for coming tonight," Travis added, shooting a smile at George.

The parking lot lights sent a hazy yellow over them as they scattered across the pavement, heading toward their cars. Craig's truck was just pulling out of the lot, and I noticed another car pulling in at the same time. A mud-splattered hatchback zoomed across the parking lot and pulled up to the curb right next to us. The passenger door swung open practically before the car stopped. I did a double take when I saw who got out.

"Brad! You're coming to practice *now*?" I asked.

Brad yanked his gym bag out after him. "Better late than never," he said. I noticed he wasn't exactly dressed to play. He wore the same dirt-stained clothes he'd had on before, except that now they were even dirtier. Fresh mud on his sneakers left wet stains on the concrete as he started toward the gym doors.

Just before he reached them, the doors pushed open and Coach Stanislaus came out. He was followed by the rest of the guys on the Cedar Plains team. The coach scowled when he saw Brad.

"You'd better have a good reason why you missed tonight's training session, Fogler," the coach said. He turned to gaze at the hatchback as it pulled away from the curb. "And I can tell you right now that joyriding with your girlfriend is *not* an acceptable excuse."

As the hatchback passed beneath one of the lights, I caught sight of the driver's high cheekbones and braids pulled back in a ponytail. Bess must have seen too, because she turned to Brad and said, "You were out with *Tanya*?"

"She's not my girlfriend or anything," he said quickly. "We were just, um—"

"Save the excuses," Coach Stanislaus said, cutting him off. "Be here on time for our next practice, or you're suspended from the team."

Brad stared moodily down at his feet as the coach and the other guys continued on. Just Brad, Bess, George, and I were left standing there.

"We might as well head home," I said, starting toward George's car.

"Would you mind taking the wheel?" George asked me, holding out her keys. "I'm just so beat."

"No problem." I was pretty tired myself, but I could handle the short drive. I grabbed the keys from George, and then noticed that Bess wasn't following us. She stood frowning in the direction of Tanya's car.

"Earth to Bess," George called. "What's the matter?"

"Well," Bess said slowly, "Tanya told me she couldn't stay late to work at the foundry because something important came up. But . . ." She shot a sideways glance at Brad's face and clothes. "You look like you were stomping around in a giant mud puddle. What's so important about that?"

Brad slung the strap of his gym bag over his shoulder. He headed toward the car without looking at Bess or answering her question. "Let's just go home," he muttered.

Bess raised an eyebrow at me. "Why won't he say where they were?" she whispered.

We tried to ask Brad about it again, but he just slumped against the backseat and stared out the window. "You don't need to know everything about my life," he said.

He didn't say much as we headed down River Street toward River Heights. He just stared out the window—until we started talking about watching the Bullets play. Glancing at him in the rearview mirror, I was sure I saw a spark of interest in his eyes. I couldn't resist trying once more to get him to talk to us.

"I was surprised you weren't there, Brad," I said. "I mean, you live for basketball. Why would you miss out on training with the best team in the state?"

"I wanted to, but . . . ," he began. He seemed to

soften, but in the next instant the angry mask was back. "I just couldn't, that's all," he said.

"Look out for that car, Nancy!" George spoke up suddenly from the passenger seat.

My eyes snapped from the rearview mirror to the road in front of me—just in time to see an oncoming car swerve across the road in front of us as it turned onto a side street. I slammed on the brakes just in time, and we all jolted against our shoulder belts.

"Whoa!" I said.

"Cutting it a little close, isn't he?" George muttered, staring at the car's glowing red taillights. I was about to hit the gas again when she said, "Hey, isn't that the way to the foundry?"

I glanced toward the side of the road, and sure enough, there was the battered old sign among the evergreens. "That's weird. Why would someone go up there this time of night?" I wondered.

George looked at Bess in the backseat, and they both shrugged. I didn't wait for an answer. Pressing down on the gas pedal, I spun the wheel to the right.

"Hang on, guys," I said. "We're going to find out."

8

Night Chase

The car shot through the trees on the narrow drive. Except for our headlights, the road was completely dark. Shadowy trees arched overhead like dark, sinister figures. The other car had already disappeared around the first bend in the road. I pressed the gas pedal a little more, and we flew around the curve.

"Careful," George cautioned. She gripped her seat as the outside tires spun on the muddy shoulder before finding the road again.

The headlights of the other car swooped in a wide arc ahead of us, then disappeared around another turn. I didn't want to get too close, but I was also concerned about losing the car from my field of vision. As I edged closer, the other car suddenly revved its engine, picking up speed. It flew around the next turn with screeching tires, sending mud flying out behind it.

"Looks like he figured out we're following him," Bess said, leaning forward in the backseat. "Just don't kill us trying to keep up with him!"

I eased up slightly on the accelerator. I didn't dare take my eyes off the road—not with those sharp curves coming fast and furious. We were rising up toward the cliffs, with each bend taking us higher. The other car was about thirty feet in front of us, but it was gaining distance every second.

"Can you guys see the license plate?" I asked. "Or even what kind of car it is?"

I groaned as we lost sight of it again. I could still hear its roaring engine, but for the next few bends in the road it stayed out of sight ahead of us.

"Finally!" I said as we emerged from the trees and saw the foundry.

In one quick glance I took in the hulking dark silhouette of the old factory. The only lights were a pair of industrial lamps outside the big double doors. I didn't see the headlights of the other car anywhere.

"Weird," said George, looking around. "Where'd the other car go?"

I slowed the car to a stop at the corner of the

parking lot closest to the foundry. The lot was so dark, it looked like a vast, inky pool surrounded by an even darker wall of trees.

"Someone should tell Owen to put up a few lights," George muttered. "I can't see a—"

Vroom!

A car engine revved deafeningly, and there was a blinding flash of light behind us. We all spun in our seats—just in time to see the other car shoot out of sight down the narrow drive toward River Street.

"He tricked us!" Brad said indignantly.

I was already pulling my car around to follow, but by the time we reached River Street, the other car was gone. The road was deserted as far as we could see in either direction. Pulling to the side of the road, I reached into my bag for my cell phone.

"I'm calling Chief McGinnis," I said. "I don't know why I didn't think of it before. After all that happened today, he should definitely have officers patrolling the foundry."

Chief McGinnis took my call a few moments later, but he didn't sound thrilled to hear my voice.

"Yes, Nancy? What is it this time?" he asked.

He was never really thrilled to hear from me, probably because of my habit of showing him up every now and then. But, hey, it's not my fault that I've solved a few crimes that baffled his squad. Dad says Chief McGinnis should be thankful, but he's usually a bit short-tempered with me. Tonight was no exception. When I told him about the sabotage to the renovation project and the car we'd just chased, the chief's first reaction was a long, weary sigh.

"What makes you so sure the other car didn't just make a wrong turn, Nancy?" he asked.

"The guy turned off his lights to trick us," I explained. "Trust me, Chief McGinnis, no one with good intentions drives that fast on such a windy little road. What if he was planning to wreck more of the work we did at the foundry?"

The chief seemed to think this over. "Well . . . my squad is spread thin as it is," he said after a moment. "We've got cars helping the Cedar Plains police make sure there's no trouble in flooded zones. But I'll have my men drive up to the foundry whenever they can."

"And you'll post a guard there full-time during the rest of the Helping Homes renovation?" I pressed.

I heard another long sigh. "I'll see what I can do, Nancy," he told me.

"I'll take that as a yes. Thanks, Chief!" I said, then closed my cell phone and dropped it back into my bag.

It was reassuring to know the police were on the lookout for trouble. At least, I *should* have been reassured. But somehow, knowing they couldn't be there every second made me worry.

As I drifted off to sleep that night, I kept imagining someone breaking windows or cutting electric wires or smashing pipes. I didn't exactly sleep soundly. Far from it. At five forty-five a.m., I opened my eyes and couldn't close them again.

No use sitting around here, I thought.

I pulled on jeans and a denim shirt and was out the door with a slice of toast and some coffee in about ten minutes. Volunteers didn't have to be at the foundry until seven, but I knew I wouldn't be able to take an easy breath until I made sure everything was all right. Getting behind the wheel of my car, I started toward the foundry.

Early commuters kept up a steady stream of traffic on River Street. My heart pounded when a Jeep a few cars ahead of me pulled off at the Davis Foundry sign. But as I made the turn behind it, I recognized the green Helping Homes logo on the side of the Jeep. Owen Jurgensen was just pulling his backpack from the rear of the Jeep when I stopped my car next to him in the foundry parking lot.

"You're here early," he said, grinning at me. "Don't

get me wrong. I'm not complaining. You can help me collect all the seam tape and joint compound we'll be using today to smooth over cracks between the pieces of Sheetrock."

"Sounds glamorous," I joked. Shading my eyes from the rising sun, I glanced up at the foundry building. "Did Chief McGinnis call you?"

Owen slung his backpack over his shoulder and swung the Jeep door shut. "Yup. He called this morning to say his men didn't see anything suspicious during their drive-by patrols last night. Starting sometime today, he's going to post a guard here around the clock." He raised an eyebrow at me as we headed toward the foundry. "I don't suppose you had anything to do with that?"

"Guilty," I admitted. I told him about the car I'd followed with Bess, George, and Brad the night before. "The chief didn't seem to think the driver was up to anything. . . ."

"But you weren't so sure?" Owen guessed.

"I'd hate to see any more of our work get wrecked, that's all," I told him.

"That makes two of us. Listen, if anything like that happens again when I'm not around, I want you to call me," Owen said. He reached into his pocket and pulled out a card, which he handed me. "This has my cell phone number."

As we reached the entrance, he unclipped a key ring from his belt. A thick knot of keys jangled while he sorted through them, then used one to open the padlock. He pulled off the heavy chain that was looped through the handles, then opened the double doors.

"Oh no," I heard him say as he stepped into the foundry ahead of me. "Not again."

I got a sinking feeling in my stomach. Glancing past Owen, I saw shards of broken ceramic scattered across the floor. They had flown outward from three sinks that lay in twisted, smashed heaps below the balcony. Looking up, I saw a half dozen more sinks standing next to some other supplies near the edge of the second-floor balcony.

"Someone pushed them from up there," I realized.

"But . . . who?" Owen wondered. "And how? The doors were locked."

I was already walking toward the stairs. "Whoever it was had to go upstairs," I said. "Maybe we'll see some kind of . . ."

I caught sight of a faint, muddy boot print on the first step. Early morning light filtered in through the windows. As I stepped back, it lit up a trail of dried prints among the shards of broken ceramic.

"The person came from that way," I said, pointing down the long hall to the right. Owen dropped his pack on the floor, and we headed that way.

The prints became clearer and thicker as we followed them down the corridor. They led us straight to the back corner apartment on the ground floor. As soon as we stepped through the doorway, I felt a cool breeze.

"Uh-oh." Owen frowned at the half-open window in the living room. Through it, we could hear the steady churning sounds of the rushing river below. "I guess we know *how* the person got in," he said.

I leaned out the window—and shuddered. The corner of the foundry came right up to the rocky cliffs. I could see over the craggy edge to the churning, rushing river fifty feet below.

"Ugh," I said, shivering. "That muddy bank is too close to the cliffs for me. Whoever climbed up here doesn't mind taking chances."

"Or getting dirty," Owen added. He nodded at the slippery mud beneath the window, at the edge of the rock.

As I stared down at the mud, an image flashed inside my head. Of Brad, covered with mud as he got out of Tanya's car the night before.

9

The Search for Secret Rooms

For a moment I just stood there staring at the muddy windowsill and floor. Questions swirled inside my head like the churning waters of the river outside.

Could Brad have anything to do with the damage to the Helping Homes renovation? Was that why he'd been acting so secretive? But then, why would he do something so destructive, especially when he and Cathy were getting one of the foundry apartments? And why would he write hate messages to J.C. Valdez? J.C. was a hero to the Cedar Plains kids.

Brad couldn't be the person in the car we'd followed, though—he'd been right with me in *George's* car. . . .

"Nancy? Did you hear me?"

Owen's voice snapped me from my thoughts. He was gazing at me expectantly from the doorway.

"Sorry," I said, shaking myself. "Um, what did you say?"

"The other volunteers will be arriving soon. Let's see if we can get those broken sinks cleared out," Owen said. "I don't want people getting spooked. If volunteers start to quit, then we'll *really* be in trouble."

He definitely had a point. "Let me just take a look up on the balcony first," I said to him. "I want to see if there are any clues to who did this."

It was already a quarter to seven. While Owen grabbed a trash bin and began throwing chunks of broken sink into it, I ran up the steps to the balcony.

"Uh-oh," I mumbled, stopping short next to the sinks. "Owen, you'd better come see this!"

I stared at the corner where the new balcony jutted up against the bricks of the old second-floor offices. When we'd left the day before, the sinks had been stored neatly next to orderly piles of plywood and boxes of tiles for the bathrooms and kitchens. Now some of the sinks lay on their side. Sheets of plywood had been pulled away from the walls and lay in a disorderly mess. Boxes of tiles had toppled to the floor. It looked as if someone had been in a hurry to get to the walls.

More precisely, to *ruin* the walls. Huge, ragged holes had been smashed into the newly polished bricks of the old walls. Reddish brown chunks of brick were strewn over the plywood, tiles, sinks, and floor.

"This is worse than I thought," Owen said, appearing next to me. He raked a hand through his spiked hair, his eyes grim.

My work boots scraped on gritty brick dust as I hurried over to the two holes. One was shallow and didn't break completely through the bricks. But the other one . . .

"Hey!" I said, bending close to it. I stuck my hand through the opening, stifling a sneeze as I breathed in stale-smelling, dusty air. "It's another blocked-off room!"

"*Another* one?"

Owen was next to me in about three nanoseconds. We stared into the dark, dusty space. Like the other walled-off space we'd found, this one was filled with cobwebs and dust balls. I saw the outline of a doorway that had been covered over with cinder blocks at some point—years before, judging by the layers of cobwebs and dust on the walls, ceiling, and floor. In the dim light that filtered through the hole, I spotted scraping footsteps on the dusty floor and more holes that had been smashed into the inside walls of the little room.

I was definitely sensing a pattern here, right down to the silver spray paint. There on the inside wall was another dripping message:

VALDEZ STINKS

"Just like yesterday," Owen said. He took a breath and let it out in a frustrated rush. "I thought it would be good for Helping Homes to have J.C. working with us. Now I'm starting to wonder...."

Owen's cool, can-do attitude was starting to crack. Seeing how worried he was, I was even more determined to stop the person who'd caused the damage. "It's weird," I said, thinking out loud. "Whoever did this couldn't have uncovered *two* secret rooms by accident. Something else is going on. Something more than just trying to hurt Helping Homes—or J.C. Valdez."

"Well, the damage *is* hurting us, whether that was what the person intended or not," Owen said. He turned away from the ragged hole and glanced down toward the lobby. We heard the double doors opening, then voices exclaiming over the smashed sinks.

"I'd like to try to find out more about these hidden spaces," I said. "Why don't I head over to the Historical Society to talk to Luther Eldridge right now? He knows more about the foundry than anyone else."

Owen was already starting down the stairs, but he paused to glance back at me. "Well, all right," he said reluctantly. "But come back as soon as you can. I need every pair of hands I can get!"

I pulled up in front of the River Heights Historical Society about fifteen minutes later. Cathy's Catered Table van was parked right in front of me. I was surprised to see an RH News truck there too, as well as Deirdre Shannon's bright pink, two-seat convertible.

Inside, Cathy and Hannah were busy setting up a breakfast buffet of coffee, juice, cereal, and cinnamon rolls. At least, they were *trying* to; the room was so crowded, it was hard to move. J.C. Valdez, Travis, and a handful of their teammates were milling about the tables, talking with flood victims. Deirdre was pelting the RH News reporter with instructions. She kept bumping into Cathy and Hannah as she pulled the cameraman around with her.

"Be sure to get some close-ups of J.C. Valdez—and me, of course," Deirdre was saying. "Viewers should know all we're doing to lift people's spirits after those horrible floods."

"Why don't you let me direct the cameraman, Miss Shannon?" the reporter suggested dryly.

"As long as you people get it right," Deirdre said curtly. "J.C. is handing out Bullets basketballs to the kids. Is your cameraman getting that? Excuse me! You, there, with the coffee. You're in the way."

Hannah rolled her eyes as she finished handing out coffee mugs around the two long tables. Ignoring Deirdre, she stepped in front of the camera on her way to join Cathy and me by the buffet table. She leveled a critical look at J.C., who grinned for the camera while he handed out basketballs to some boys and girls.

"I know everyone loves a sports star. But if you ask me, that boy loves his own fame more than any person ought to," she said. She gave a knowing shake of her gray-haired head. "He's just like my cousin Peter after he won the hot-dog-eating contest at the state fair. He was insufferable!"

"He and Deirdre *do* seem to like the cameras a lot," I agreed. "Owen Jurgensen won't be happy that J.C. and the guys are late this morning, but at least they're cheering up the kids," I said.

I chuckled as Deirdre elbowed her way in next to J.C., but my smile faded when I saw the distracted, worried expression on Cathy's face. She was just bringing a cinnamon roll and a glass of juice to the elderly, white-haired man I'd seen talking with Brad two days earlier. He was still going on about his dog, but Cathy didn't seem to be listening very closely.

I had a feeling I knew what was bothering her.

"Cathy's still worried about Brad?" I asked Hannah.

"As if she doesn't have enough to think about—losing her home and trying to keep her business together," Hannah said. "I don't know what's troubling that boy—sneaking off at odd hours. And when he *is* home, he barely talks to your father or Cathy or me."

I decided not to mention Brad's mud-stained clothes or the muddy prints Owen and I had discovered at the foundry. At least, not until I had more information to go on.

"Um, have you seen Mr. Eldridge? I need to ask him something," I said.

"I think I saw him go into his office," Hannah told me. She pointed to a door at the back of the library, set in among the bookshelves that lined the wall. The door was ajar, and through the opening, I saw Luther Eldridge sitting behind his desk. A moment later I pushed the door open wide, and Luther smiled up from his newspaper.

"What took you so long, Nancy?" he asked

"Excuse me?" I asked.

"Owen Jurgensen called yesterday to tell me about the photographs that were stolen from the foundry," Luther said. "I figured it wouldn't be long before you'd come around asking about them. I've had the originals ready for you to look at since yesterday afternoon. They're right over there."

"Am I that predictable?" I asked, laughing.

"Just thorough," Luther told me. Getting up, he gestured to a table next to the window. On it, I saw two black-and-white photographs in protective plastic sleeves. Next to them was a building floor plan, yellowed with age and cracked at the edges.

"Actually, just two of the things taken were photographs," Luther explained. "The third was a framed photocopy of this floor plan. It dates from nineteen twenty-seven."

"Of course!" I said, smacking my forehead. "I wondered what the stolen photos had to do with the damage. Whoever took the floor plan must have used it to find the secret rooms!" I looked at the floor plan. "Does it show any parts of the original factory that were sealed off?" I asked.

"Sealed off? Sure," he told me. "The Davis Foundry was altered several times over the years, to suit the changing needs of the factory. It wouldn't have been unusual for odd spaces to be sealed off if they didn't serve a purpose any longer," he said.

I was already poring over the plan. "Here . . . and here," I said, pinpointing the two hidden rooms the person had broken into. "It looks like this one on the first floor was blocked off when something called a stamping room was created."

Luther looked down at the plan and nodded. "Mmm. The Davis Foundry began making metal signs about that time," Luther said. He gazed down at the second hidden space I pointed to, next to the old second-floor offices. "And that was walled over when storage space was converted to new offices."

"Uh-huh. So what's the big deal about those little rooms?" I murmured, thinking out loud. "Why is someone busting through to them after all this time?" I tapped my fingers against the yellowed floor plan, wishing an explanation would jump out at me, but none did.

With a sigh, I picked up the photographs in their protective sleeves. One showed a crew of men pouring molten metal into some kind of mold, with the big Davis Foundry clock visible on the wall above them. The second showed a row of men in suits standing on a platform overlooking a vast room filled with huge machines, stacks of metal sheets, and coils of some shiny metal.

"That's Mr. Kenneth C. Davis himself," Luther said, pointing to the stout, bearded man at the center. "I'm not sure of the exact date, but it's sometime around nineteen fifty-five. Mr. Davis closed the factory not long after this. There was quite a scandal surrounding the closing, actually."

"Really?" I said.

"There was a theft at the foundry. A half million dollars in cash was taken from the safe in Mr. Davis's office," Luther explained. He pointed at a photographed image of the man who stood to Mr. Davis's left. "That's Bernard Tilden, Mr. Davis's accountant. Police were fairly certain it was he who took the money."

"Fairly certain? They didn't arrest him?" I asked.

Luther shook his head. "Tilden died in a car crash before they could. The money was never found."

I bit my lip, staring at the grainy black-and-white image of Bernard Tilden. He was taller and thinner than Mr. Davis. He wore glasses, and his shirtsleeves were rolled up, as if he were used to hunkering down and working hard.

"I wonder . . . what if *that's* why someone's wrecking walls and punching holes into sealed-off rooms?" I murmured. "The person could be looking for the missing money. . . ."

"What's this about missing money?" a voice spoke up at the doorway.

I turned to see J.C. Valdez standing there. His smile faded as he saw the photographs I was holding.

"There was another attack at the foundry last night," I told him. "Someone likes putting holes in walls—and writing not-so-nice things about you."

"Again?" J.C. frowned and shoved his hands in his pants pockets. "Craig doesn't know when to stop, does he?"

"If it was him," I said. "Anyway, I figured it couldn't hurt to find out about the photographs that were stolen yesterday."

"Nancy was just wondering if the damage to the foundry might have something to do with some money that was stolen from the factory a good many years back," Luther put in. "The man who took the money is in one of the photos that was taken from the foundry."

"Really?" A spark of interest lit up J.C.'s eyes, and he came over to look at the photo.

I wasn't sure why, but I wished Luther hadn't mentioned the stolen money. Call me cautious, but I don't usually share my investigations with just anyone. J.C. Valdez was nice enough. But the intense curiosity in his eyes made me uncomfortable.

"I guess it's pretty unlikely," I said quickly. "I mean, why would anyone think the money is still in the factory? The place closed more than fifty years ago. If someone *was* going to look for the money, they would have done it a long time ago."

J.C. nodded, his eyes on the yellowed building plan on the table. "Besides," he added, "why would a person who's looking for money bother to write hate messages about me?"

I took a deep breath and let it out slowly. "I'll have to add that to my list of questions," I said. "Too bad I still don't have any answers."

10

Friends—or Foes?

Hold up a sec. Something doesn't feel right," Bess said.

It was that evening, and she, George, and I had just gotten out of my car in front of Deirdre Shannon's house. A string of cars lined the road ahead of us. People in jackets, ties, dresses, and heels flowed up the walk—lined with colorful Chinese lanterns—toward the front door. The night air was filled with laughter, talking, and music, but I agreed with Bess.

"I've got a weird feeling too," I said, smoothing the skirt of my wraparound dress. "I don't think I'll be in much of a party mood until I figure out what the attacks on the foundry are all about—and who's responsible."

"Oh, I'm in a party mood. I was talking about

something else." Bess arched a teasing eyebrow at me and gestured to the couple strolling up the curved walk ahead of us. "Where's all the plaster dust? Where are the work boots and bandannas and hammers and saws and plywood and pipes? I've gotten so used to that stuff that it feels strange to be around people wearing nice clothes and makeup."

"Plaster dust and work boots aren't exactly Deirdre's style," George said, rolling her eyes. "Anyway, it'll be fun to hang out with everyone *away* from a construction site for a change. I mean, even all those bad floods shouldn't stop us from having a good time, right?"

Leave it to Bess and George to stop me from taking things too seriously. After all, why shouldn't we have fun tonight? Lighten up, Drew, I told myself sternly.

But as we headed inside, my mind was still on all the questions I had about the attacks on the foundry. Why had the person broken through to those two sealed-off rooms? There had to be a reason, but I couldn't think of what it was. And what about J.C.? Were the attacks aimed at him? Was Craig behind them, the way J.C. claimed? Was there a reason those particular photographs and floor plan had been taken—or had the person just grabbed any old things at random?

Then there was the biggest question on my mind, the one I hated even to consider.

"Have you guys seen Brad or Tanya?" I asked Bess and George.

George shot a surprised glance at me as we made our way into the living room. "You *really* think they had something to do with last night's break-in at the foundry?" she asked.

I shrugged, gazing at the swarming, jumping, swaying people who were dancing. Someone waved, and it took me a second to make out Owen—in a black jacket, slate gray crew-neck shirt, and pleated trousers—dancing with a bunch of volunteers. I smiled back, but I wasn't quite ready to join them yet.

"Brad didn't give me a chance to talk to him today," I said to George and Bess. "Owen kept us all busy after I got back from the Historical Society. Brad worked straight through lunch, and when I tried to talk to him, he said he was too busy. The second Owen told us to quit for the day, Brad took off, so I couldn't talk to him then, either."

"And now he's not here," George added. "At least, not that I can see."

As we looked around, I saw some of the guys from Brad's team dancing with Owen and the other volunteers. Travis and some of the other Bullets were there too. But not Brad.

So much for lightening up. "I really hope he didn't have anything to do with the attacks," Bess said. "And Tanya, too. I mean, she worked just as hard as anyone on our team today. And she's so nice. . . . I just can't believe she had anything to do with the attacks on the foundry."

The blinding flash of a camera made me blink. I looked through the arched doorway to the dining room buffet. I groaned when I saw Deirdre and J.C. Valdez smiling for a photographer from the *River Heights Bugle*. The two of them barreled past us a moment later, heading for the dance floor.

"You promised your first dance to me, remember?" Deirdre said coyly.

"I'm all yours," J.C. told her. "For a while, anyway. I'm going to have to leave early to drive over to my parents' new house in Woodburn."

"But you're the guest of honor! Can't you go tomorrow?" Deirdre said, pouting.

J.C. smiled apologetically. "It's an hour away. You wouldn't want me to break a promise to my mom, would you?" he said.

Deirdre didn't look very happy, but she didn't complain as J.C. led her to the dance floor. As they started dancing, he shimmied close to her, then angled a smug look back toward the buffet.

That was when I noticed Craig Reynolds. He stood holding a plate of shrimp, watching J.C. and Deirdre with hooded eyes.

"If you ask me, Craig's the one you should be keeping an eye on," Bess said. "Not Brad and Tanya. Oh, there's Tanya now!"

She pointed toward the far end of the buffet, where Tanya stood in a red dress with fringe at the hem and a rainbow-striped scarf wrapped around her braids. She grinned when she saw us.

"Those seafood pastry puffs are to die for," Tanya said, pointing to a tray on the buffet.

Bess took a plate, but as she reached for the little pastries, I turned to Tanya. "Could we talk? Someplace that's not so crowded?" I asked.

Tanya met my gaze with steady eyes. "Sure," she said. She nodded toward some French doors that led to a patio outside. "How about out there?"

Bess and George followed as we made our way outside. Chinese lanterns hung along the edges of the patio, but the garden beyond was shrouded in shadows. There was a chill in the air that made goose bumps pop out on my arms.

"Brad told me you were asking where we were last night," Tanya said, closing the French doors behind us. "Is that what this is about?"

"Sort of." My heels clicked on the slate as I walked

over to one of the patio chairs and sat down. "Whoever broke into the foundry last night got in through a window next to the cliffs. There were muddy prints inside."

"What does that have to do with Brad and me?" Tanya asked, taking the chair next to mine.

I took a deep breath before answering. "Brad was totally muddy when you dropped him off at Cedar Plains High," I said.

Tanya stared at me, then shook her head. "You think *we* snuck in and smashed those sinks? That's crazy!"

"I tried to tell you, Nancy," Bess began.

"I have to consider every possibility," I said quickly. "And since Brad wouldn't tell me what you two were doing—"

"You figured we were out wrecking the apartments we're all trying so hard to build?" Tanya snapped. Her eyes flashed angrily as she turned from me to Bess to George. "Do you really think I'd do anything to hurt all the work Helping Homes is doing? Or that Brad would?"

It *was* hard to picture either of them doing anything so destructive. Brad was practically like family to Dad and me! Still, I couldn't squelch the niggling doubts in my mind. "Just tell us what you were doing, then," I said.

Tanya's eyes flitted uncertainly over the garden for a long moment before she spoke. "I can't do that," she said at last.

"Why not?" Bess asked, staring in surprise at Tanya.

"I just can't. You'll have to trust Brad and me, that's all," Tanya said. "We didn't have anything to do with all the stuff that happened at the foundry."

Tanya got to her feet. "Let's just forget about this and have fun, okay?" she said, shooting a tentative smile at us. "Anyone up for some dancing?"

"Count me in!" Bess answered. She headed for the French doors, and George followed.

"Me too. Coming, Nancy?" she said, raising an eyebrow at me.

"In a minute," I told them.

The click of the closing doors echoed in the cool night. I definitely needed some time to think. Stepping off the patio, I moved into the calm, quiet shadows of the garden. As my eyes adjusted to the darkness, I made out shadowy clumps of shrubs and flowers and a wall of hedges along the perimeter. I walked alongside the hedge, breathing in the smell of freshly cut grass.

Tanya had asked us to trust her, but could we? I replayed our conversation in my mind. Tanya acted genuinely shocked that we would suspect her of any wrongdoing. Still, if she and Brad *hadn't* been up to anything suspicious, why wouldn't she talk about what they *had* done? It just didn't seem possible that—

I stopped short, suddenly aware of a rustling in the hedges.

"Hello?" I said. "Bess? George? Is that you?"

I stood still, listening. At first all I heard was the pounding of my own heart. Then there was something more—the swish of a foot brushing across the grass.

"Who's there?" I called sharply.

I waited for an answer. But all I heard were the steady sounds of breathing coming from the other side of the hedge.

11

A Clue in the Night

W ho is it?" I said again, though my voice didn't sound nearly as firm as I'd intended. All at once I was hyperaware of how dark and deserted the Shannons' garden was.

Get a grip! I told myself.

A sudden rustling on the other side of the hedge shocked me into action. I heard rapid, thumping footsteps—whoever was there had taken off, heading farther into the garden.

"No way. You're not getting away that easily," I said under my breath.

Pushing off with my heels, I took off in the same direction. The thick hedges blocked my view, but snapping, rustling branches told me I wasn't far behind whoever was on the other side.

Suddenly, a dark shadow burst through a break in the hedge ahead of me. The person moved so fast that all I saw was a blur shooting past shadowy clumps of flowers and the chunky silhouette of some kind of urn.

"Drat!" I groaned as I stumbled on my heels. I yanked them off, but when I looked up again, the quick-moving shadow was disappearing around the far edge of the garden.

Clutching my shoes, I sped in the same direction. As I rounded the corner of the Shannons' house, I heard music inside, but my eyes stayed glued to the shrubs and trees in front of me. I couldn't help wishing the Shannons' landscaping wasn't quite so elaborate. I had totally lost sight of the person among the greenery.

Where *are* you? I thought, tearing around to the front of the house. Breathing hard, I scanned the front yard. The Chinese lanterns lit up the neatly trimmed grass—and a solitary figure standing at the curb. He turned slightly, and I saw his face in the colorful glow.

"Craig?" I said.

The red paper lantern made his hair look more fiery than usual. Stepping between two cars, he stared at the glowing taillights of a car that was disappearing down the road.

I caught up to him a moment later. "What are you doing out here?" I asked, trying to catch my breath.

"Huh?" Craig flinched as I touched his arm. He turned toward me, and I saw that he was breathing hard. Bits of grass stuck to his shoes. He glanced distractedly at me before staring back down the road. "I, uh . . . just came out to get some air," he said.

"By sprinting through the garden?" I stepped between the cars and planted myself in front of him. "Were you eavesdropping on my friends and me?" I asked.

"Friends? I don't see any friends," Craig looked pointedly at the empty space behind me, then nodded at my grass-covered feet and the shoes in my hand. "Anyway, looks like *you're* the one who's been running through the garden."

I stifled a groan. The guy obviously wasn't going to give me a straight answer. "I was chasing someone who . . ."

My voice trailed off as I spotted something in the shadow of the parked car right next to us. It was small and rectangular—maybe a book? It lay on the pavement a few feet from Craig's feet. Hmm, I thought. Had he dropped it?

"Someone who what?" Craig asked me, an impatient edge in his voice.

"Someone who, um . . ." I let one of my shoes fall to

the pavement. Maybe it wasn't the most original ploy in the world, but I hoped Craig would buy it. "Oops!" I said, bending to pick up my shoe. Just before grabbing it, I quickly scooped up the object I'd spotted. My fingers closed around a small leather notebook. I slipped it up my sleeve and then straightened up again, keeping my back to Craig.

"Never mind. I guess I was wrong," I said, flashing him a smile over my shoulder. "Sorry to bother you."

I hurried back up the walk to the house, clutching the shoes—and notebook—in front of me. Just before I went in, I glanced over my shoulder and saw Craig staring after me. I slipped inside, shut the door behind me, and wound through the crowd until I found George and Bess dancing in the living room.

"What's with the bare feet?" Bess asked.

With so many people jammed in close to us, I didn't want to talk about what had happened.

"I'll tell you later," I said. Then, dropping the notebook quickly into my bag, I put my shoes back on and started to dance.

"I can't wait anymore. Show us that book you found, Nancy!" George said.

She leaned over our table at Scoops, our favorite ice-cream place, and used a straw to stir her chocolate milk shake. All our dancing at Deirdre's had made us hungry, and we figured Scoops was as good a place as any to look at the notebook I'd picked up.

"It's right here," I told her. Sticking my spoon into the banana split Bess and I were sharing, I pulled the little notebook from my bag.

"Craig dropped it, huh?" Bess said. Taking the leather book from me, she fingered the cover. "It looks pretty old. Check out how worn and cracked the leather is."

"Not to mention smelly." George crinkled up her nose in distaste. "There's mildew on the cover—like it's been sitting in some dank basement." She leaned closer as Bess opened the cover.

"It's a journal," Bess said, reading the slanted writing on the yellowed page. "The guy wrote his name: Bernard Tilden. And there's the date. Nineteen fifty-five."

"Bernard Tilden?" The name definitely rang a bell—then I had it. "He was the accountant at the Davis Foundry!"

"The one Mr. Eldridge said stole all that money?" Bess glanced up from the old book, her eyes wide. "Maybe he wrote about it in his journal!"

"Well, don't just sit there. Read!" George urged.

Bess began turning the pages, scanning each one.

"Hmm. This is just a bunch of notes keeping track of clients and invoices and stuff," she said.

"Nothing more personal?" I asked.

Bess bit her lip and turned a few more crinkled pages. "More records and figures . . . oh, wait. Here's something," she murmured.

She ran her finger along the slanted words in the journal. "'Showed KD annual report and earnings statement,'" she read. "'KD disappointed in figures. Warned not to expect bonuses this year. Hardly seems fair after all my hard work.'"

She arched an eyebrow at George and me. "He sounds a little bitter, doesn't he?" she said. "Who's KD?"

"Kenneth Davis was the president of the Davis Foundry," I told her. "He must be KD."

George nodded, slurping up some shake through her straw. "Does he write anything else?" she asked.

"Let's see . . ." Bess turned back to the journal and flipped ahead. "He makes a few more comments about not feeling appreciated, but I don't see . . . oh my gosh, listen to this!"

She jabbed a finger at the middle of a page and read. "'KD critical of this month's figures. Hinted sloppy bookkeeping is to blame.'"

"That doesn't sound fair," I said, scooping some

ice cream, bananas, and sauce with my spoon. "If the company was doing badly, it wasn't necessarily Tilden's fault."

"According to this, Bernard Tilden agreed with you, Nan," Bess told me. "He decided to get back at Mr. Davis. He actually stole some things from him!"

I nearly choked on a mouthful of banana split. "Money?" I said after I had managed to swallow. "Say, a half million dollars?"

"There's nothing about that here," Bess said, shaking her head. "But he *did* take Mr. Davis's watch and a box of Cuban cigars. He also took the Davis Foundry seal—sounds like some kind of official stamp for papers and stuff. Here's what he wrote." She cleared her throat and then read, "'KD owes me for all I've done. If he can't show his appreciation, then I'll simply take what I deserve.'"

"Sounds like he's getting bolder," George commented.

"And sneakier. Like maybe he's planning an even bigger theft," I added.

Bess kept turning pages, skimming them as she went. After a few moments she looked up with wide eyes. "Bingo," she said.

She pointed to one of the entries, turning the journal so that George and I could read it:

OVERHEARD KD ON THE PHONE. BANK SENDING
ARMORED TRUCK ON FRIDAY FOR $$$ IN THE
VAULT. IF ALL GOES AS I PLAN, THE $$$
WILL NEVER MAKE IT TO THE BANK.

"So he *did* plan to steal the money," George
breathed out.

"Oh, he did more than just plan," Bess told us.
"Look!"

She pointed to the next entry, and George and I
bent close to read:

MY PLAN WENT LIKE CLOCKWORK. KD CALLS MY
WORK SLOPPY, BUT TODAY IT WAS FLAWLESS.
BETTER THAN FLAWLESS! THE OLD FOOL DOESN'T
EVEN SUSPECT THAT HIS VAULT IS NOW EMPTY
AND THAT ITS CONTENTS ARE RIGHT UNDER HIS
NOSE, IN A ROOM LONG FORGOTTEN BY EVERYONE
BUT ME. BY THE TIME HE REALIZES THE $$$
IS GONE, I WILL BE FAR AWAY WITH IT.

I turned the page to read on, but it was blank.
"That's it. It's the last thing he wrote," I said.

A wild excitement buzzed through me. "Mr.
Eldridge told me that Bernard Tilden died in a car

crash before police could arrest him." I looked across the table at Bess and George. "What if he died *before* he had a chance to get the money out of that long-forgotten room he wrote about?"

"Then the money could still be there!" Bess said.

"Whoever dropped this," I said, closing the cracked leather cover, "knows all about it. And he's been tearing up the foundry trying to find the secret room with the money in it!"

"Well, it's pretty clear who it is, then," George said. She drained the last of her milk shake, then stared at me over the top of her glass. "Craig Reynolds must be the guy we're after."

12

Follow Them!

I had a tough time sleeping that night. Every time I closed my eyes, I pictured Craig Reynolds staring down the street with Bernard Tilden's notebook at his feet. Craig *had* to be the person who was going after the money. Still, nagging thoughts pricked me like needles. If Craig was trying to find the hidden money, why would he write slurs against J.C.? Even if he was bitter about J.C.'s success, he wouldn't want to call attention to himself.

Would he?

And what about Brad and Tanya? I wanted to believe what Tanya had said about her and Brad not doing anything to hurt the foundry, but every time I pictured Brad's muddy clothes and shoes, I had my doubts. I couldn't shake the feeling that I was missing something—that some piece of the puzzle just didn't fit right. . . .

Brinng!

My alarm jolted me from an uneasy sleep. Ugh. Six o'clock already? I thought.

I dragged myself out of bed, barely able to open my eyes. Luckily, we detectives have a secret recipe for shaking off the cobwebs so we can look at a case with fresh eyes. It's called a shower. Five minutes under the steamy spray, and I felt ready for anything.

"Brad!" I said as I walked into the kitchen in my jeans, T-shirt, and bandanna.

I had gotten so used to his disappearing acts that it was a surprise to see him sitting at the kitchen table. A glass of OJ and a plate of barely touched toast sat in front of him. His hair was tousled, and there were rings under his eyes—as if he hadn't slept well either.

"I didn't see you at the Shannons' party last night," I said.

Brad just shrugged. "So?" he said, without looking at me.

"I'm surprised that you're not spending as much time as you can with the Bullets, that's all," I told him. "I mean, we're lucky to have them around, but it seems like you're *avoiding* hanging around with them—and blowing off work with Helping Homes."

Brad frowned down at his toast. "Look, I got enough lectures from Coach Stanislaus. I don't need one from you, too," he said. "I'm going to the foundry right on time today, so you can back off, okay?"

I poured myself some coffee and leaned against the counter facing Brad. "I know you wouldn't normally pass up the chance to train with the Bullets," I tried again.

"Nothing about my life is normal these days, in case you hadn't noticed," Brad shot back. "I lost my house, my whole neighborhood is covered with mud. . . . So why don't you just leave me alone."

Angry sparks shot from his eyes as he shoved his chair back, stood up, and grabbed his car keys from the counter. He stormed to the back door, and it slammed behind him a moment later.

I stared after him, cradling my mug in my hands. Okay, so I wasn't going to get any straight answers out of Brad. I hoped to do better with Craig Reynolds. After digging around in my bag for the card Owen Jurgensen had given me, I picked up my phone and called him.

"This is Owen. Talk to me!" his voice came over the line.

I gave him a quick rundown of what had happened the night before. But when I told him that I wanted to follow up on Craig right away, he cut me off.

"I need every volunteer, Nancy," Owen said sternly. "We're way behind schedule as it is. I can't have you traipsing off and missing important work time. Why don't you wait a few hours? At least until we break for lunch."

I hesitated, but Owen didn't give me a chance to say no.

"Look, if Craig Reynolds *is* the guy you're after," he said, "he'll come back to the foundry to look for the money again. You really need to be here so you can keep a lookout in case he tries anything."

"Okay, okay," I finally agreed. "I'll be there in about fifteen minutes."

"Help me with this tape, okay, Nancy?" George said.

I tucked a strand of hair under my Helping Homes hat and turned back to the wall George and I were working on. I had just used a trowel to spread a thin layer of plaster over the seam between two pieces of wallboard. The next step—as Wilson had shown us—was to cover the seam with a wide strip of paper tape. After that we'd smooth over the seam with more plaster, and when the plaster dried, we would sand it. When we were done, the seams would be totally hidden, so that each wall would have a smooth, perfect surface.

That was how it worked in theory, anyway. But I have to admit, I was distracted.

"Um, Nancy? You missed a spot," George told me. "What's so interesting outside, anyway?"

"Sorry," I said, turning away from the window. I scraped more wet plaster from the bottom of the bucket and quickly spread it over the paper tape George had placed on the seam. "I just wanted to make sure the guard is still there."

"Officer Brandt? He was there the last twenty times you checked," George teased. "And there haven't been any attacks on the foundry today."

I was definitely glad about that, but somehow, I still couldn't concentrate on what we were doing. "I guess I'm just impatient to find out more about Craig and the money Bernard Tilden stole," I admitted. I glanced at my watch and sighed. "We've got more than an hour to go before we break for lunch. . . ."

The other volunteers on our team were out of sight in other rooms of the apartment, but we could hear them talking and laughing while they worked. George and I were taping seams in the back bedroom of one of the second-floor apartments. From the window, I could see Officer Brandt. He walked along the riverbank, keeping his eyes on the factory, then turned toward the blue tarp where construction materials were stored. As I watched, a flash of movement beyond the tarp caught my eye. I turned for a closer look—then frowned.

"How come Brad and Tanya are leaving?" I murmured.

"Now? After Owen gave that speech this morning about working together to make up for lost time?" George bent close to the window. We watched as Brad and Tanya walked toward the parking lot from the foundry. Maybe it was my imagination, but I could have sworn I saw Brad look furtively over his shoulder before he got into Tanya's hatchback.

I dropped my trowel into the empty plaster bucket and jammed the top on. "I know I promised Owen I'd stay here, but someone's got to follow them."

"Well, if you're going, I'm going too," George said, putting down her roll of paper tape.

J.C., Travis, Cam, and Wilson all looked up as as we hurried through the living room of the apartment. "Everything all right?" Wilson asked.

"Yeah. We just have to, um . . . ," George began.

"Get more plaster!" I fibbed. "We'll be back in a minute." We didn't bother waiting for an answer, but ran down the hall to the stairs.

"A minute? Something tells me we'll be gone a

little longer than that," George said under her breath as we took the stairs two at a time.

I just pushed open the doors and hurried outside. "Come on! We've got to catch up to them before they get to River Street."

We were in luck. We rounded the last curve in the drive in time to see Tanya's hatchback turn onto River Street.

"She's going left," George said.

I let Tanya's car cruise down the road some before I turned after it. "It looks like they going toward Cedar Plains," I said.

George nodded, keeping her eyes on the car ahead. "Maybe Brad has to get something at the high school?" she guessed.

But when Tanya reached the turnoff for Cedar Plains High, she drove straight past it. I thought she might stop at the commercial strip in downtown Cedar Plains, but she cruised past the stores and restaurants there, too.

"Weird," I said, frowning. "Where are they going?"

"Beats me, but check out the roadblocks," George said. She nodded to our right, at a police barrier blocking a road that dipped down behind the buildings and trees along the main road. The road just beyond was also blocked. And the next one. . . .

"The river's that way," I realized. "Those roads are probably closed because of the flooding. I guess the police haven't let anyone back there yet. It must still be too dangerous."

"Did anyone tell Brad and Tanya that?" George asked, pointing ahead. "They're going right past that one!"

Sure enough, I saw that Tanya had turned onto one of the blocked roads. Spinning the wheel of my car, I quickly pulled to the side of the road and stopped a couple dozen feet back. George and I watched as Tanya and Brad got out of the car, grabbed the ends of the police barrier, and moved it to the side of the road.

"Are they crazy? It could be dangerous back there!" I murmured. I bit my lip, frowning, as Tanya and Brad drove past the barrier. "We'd better follow them."

Putting my foot on the gas pedal, I drove slowly to the road and turned onto it. I pulled my car past the wooden barrier, then stopped so George and I could put it back in place.

"Eeew," George said, wrinkling up her nose. A sour, moldy smell was in the air. As we drove farther down the road, I saw what caused it. The floods had left a slimy layer of mud that covered everything— the road, the lawns, garbage cans, patio furniture. . . . Some houses we passed were coated with the green-

ish black slime up to the second-floor windows.

Tanya's car crept along the road ahead of us. The closer we got to the river, the more damage we saw. Trees and telephone poles had been knocked over, and entire houses had collapsed in on themselves.

"Oh, man. Talk about devastation," George said, covering her nose and mouth. "Being here in the middle of it is a thousand times worse than seeing pictures on the news. I can't believe—"

"They're stopping!" I said.

Tanya had pulled her car off the road. I did the same, stopping behind the upturned roots of a fallen maple tree half a block back. As quietly as we could, George and I got out. We could hear the rushing river not far off. For once I was glad for the noise. I was pretty sure Tanya and Brad hadn't heard us.

"It looks like they're going to that house," George whispered, peering around the muddy earth that clung to the roots of the fallen tree.

The building she pointed to was so damaged that you could hardly call it a house anymore. The roof had completely caved in on one side. The walls leaned dangerously inward, and half the windows were broken. Tanya and Brad slipped on the sour-smelling slime as they moved toward the place.

"Ugh," I said as Brad picked up a mud-coated tree branch. I thought he might use it to keep his balance on the slippery ground. But holding on to the branch, Brad crept closer and closer to the house. He walked right up to one of the windows, then angled the branch over his shoulder like a baseball bat.

"He's going to break the window!" George gasped.

Without thinking, I jumped out from behind the roots. "Stop!" I shouted. "Stop it right now!"

13

Mission in the Flood Zone

Brad and Tanya jumped about a foot in the air. They whipped around to face us, and Brad's face turned a ghostly white. He and Tanya took a step back as George and I raced toward them across the muddy ground.

"What the . . . ?" Brad said.

"Don't break that window!" I said again, slip-sliding across the slime that coated the street.

"Don't you know that's vandalism?" George added. "The floods have already done enough to the house without you two causing even more damage."

Tanya's mouth fell open. "What are you talking about?" she said. "All we're trying to do is save Mr. Fillmore's dog!"

"Dog?" I repeated. It took me a second to figure

115

out what she was talking about. "You mean the one the old guy at the Historical Society had to leave behind?"

"Otis," Brad said, nodding. "I promised Mr. Fillmore I'd try to find him."

George and I stopped and looked at each other. Now that we were closer to the house, we heard barking inside—a weak, high-pitched baying that tugged at my heart.

"The poor thing sounds like he's hurt!" I said.

"That's what we think too," Tanya said. She turned back to the house, frowning. "Whether or not it's Otis, we need to help that dog. Too bad the front door isn't exactly in good enough shape to use."

That was the understatement of the year. The front porch had half collapsed, looking like it could completely cave in at any moment.

"Which is why Brad was going to break the window?" George guessed.

"That's why you guys have been so secretive!" I realized. "You couldn't exactly tell everyone you were sneaking past police barriers." Relief washed over me—until I heard another soulful bark inside the house.

"We've got to get that dog out of there. Do you think we can get the window open without breaking it?" I suggested.

I glanced worriedly at the side of the house where we stood. It hadn't collapsed—not yet, anyway—and it didn't lean nearly as much as the other side. Stepping cautiously over to the window, I tried to open it.

"It's stuck," I said.

The next thing I knew, Brad was next to me. Together, we pushed up on the window. I was afraid it was locked, but it finally opened a crack before jamming again.

"The shifting house must have made it stick," Brad said. Gritting his teeth, he pushed up even harder—until the window screeched open about a foot.

"I can get through there," Tanya said.

"Careful." George glanced worriedly up at the outside wall of the house as Tanya strode to the window. "Can it hold your weight?"

Tanya was already stepping up onto the cradle Brad had formed with his hands. Grabbing the window ledge, she tried to shake it, but the walls remained solid. Smiling over her shoulder at us, she leaned in the window.

"It's a bulldog," she reported. "Looks like he's wedged behind an overturned table." Then I heard her croon in a soothing voice, "Otis, is that you? We're here to help you, buddy. . . ."

The dog's whining grew sharper and more urgent. Then we heard Tanya say, "I'm bringing him out.

Nothing's broken, but he's dehydrated and really weak."

A moment later she leaned out the window with a creature that was so limp, it looked more like a fur-covered rag than a dog. The dog's reddish brown fur was dull and dirty, and his breathing was shallow and rapid. The bulldog was barely able to lift his head to gaze at us with tired, red eyes.

"Oh! The poor thing," George said as Brad gently took the dog in his arms.

"I'm glad we finally found you, Otis," Brad said, stroking the dog's head. "Mr. Fillmore sure is going to be glad you're alive."

At the sound of his name the bulldog's tail wagged the slightest bit.

"See how he perked up? That's Otis, all right." George smiled as Tanya squeezed back out through the window and dropped to the ground next to us. "No wonder you guys snuck past the barriers. You couldn't just leave Otis out here to die."

Brad was heading toward Tanya's car with the bull-dog. Glancing over his shoulder at us, he said, "Mr. Fillmore was really upset about leaving Otis behind, so I promised I'd try to find him. I came by myself the first time, but—"

"Early in the morning, before our first day with Helping Homes?" I guessed.

Brad nodded. "That was when I realized how creepy it is around here," he said. "I felt weird being by myself with everything wrecked and falling down around me."

George glanced around at the fallen trees and broken-down, slimy homes. "So you asked Tanya to help you?"

"I'm glad he did too," Tanya spoke up. Opening the hatchback of her car, she spread an old blanket out. "I've had some experience with sick animals. And two of us could cover a lot more ground than one."

"It's still pretty dangerous," I said. "You two are lucky you didn't get hurt—or arrested."

Brad gently placed Otis on the blanket, talking soothingly to him all the while. When he straightened up, he said, "Well, I don't regret it. Otis is like family to Mr. Fillmore. If sneaking around was the only way to find him, I think it was the right thing to do."

"Anyway, we weren't the only ones who ignored the police barriers," Tanya added. "Just last night we saw—"

"You came here last night?" I said, taken aback. "But we saw you at Deirdre's party."

"Can't a girl have fun *and* do a good deed in one night?" Tanya said, grinning at George and me. "I met Brad afterward, and we drove down here. We almost had a heart attack when we saw J.C. Valdez walking around."

"J.C. Valdez?" George asked. She leaned against the side of Tanya's car, raising an eyebrow. "But didn't he tell Deirdre he had to leave the party early because he was going to see his parents in Woodburn?" she said.

"Definitely," I said, nodding. "That's an hour away from here, so he couldn't have been in both places."

"All I know is that Tanya and I saw him right over there," Brad said. He pointed through the piles of debris and branches to a house that stood even closer to the river.

"I wonder why he lied?" I murmured.

"Who knows," Brad said with a shrug. "Like you said, anyone who's breaking the law to come here wouldn't exactly advertise what they're doing."

"But *why* would he come here?" I said, thinking out loud.

Moving away from Tanya's car, I picked my way carefully along the muddy road toward the house. I shivered at the sight of a couple of rats scampering over the rubble of a collapsed house. Just beyond was the house Brad had pointed at. I heard Tanya's engine start, and a moment later George came up next to me.

"Brad and Tanya are taking Otis to the animal shelter," she said, trying not to slip on the mud. "They'll get him some food and water, and then they'll reintroduce him to Mr. Fillmore."

"Great," I said, still scanning the area.

I stopped next to an old wooden house that was covered with slime up to its second-story windows. Miraculously, the gabled roof and wood siding had remained intact. Even the elaborate wooden trim of the porch had survived. Not that the place looked like any sort of showcase at the moment. Trash bins lay overturned and filled with foul-smelling water. Slime-covered lawn chairs and tables were wedged against the house at odd angles. The sour stench of mold and mud made me gag.

"Maybe this is J.C.'s parents' house," I said. "Didn't J.C. tell us the house has been in his mother's family for generations?"

George nodded, gazing at the muddy walls and debris. "This place does look pretty old. It's even got one of those signs that tells about the history of the house," she said.

She pointed at a muddy wooden plaque nailed to the clapboards next to the front door. Taking a few steps closer, I peered at it. The plaque was half covered with mud, but I could still make out the words.

"George!" I breathed out. "This is the Bernard Tilden House!"

14

Race to the Stolen Money

"You're kidding!" George said, gaping at the house.

As I moved across the mud-coated walk toward the front porch, I saw skid marks in the smelly slime where someone else had walked. "It looks like J.C. went into the house. I wonder what—"

"Careful, Nan!" George said.

I had just put my foot on the steps leading up to the porch. The moldy, mud-covered board gave way with a sickening crunch. My foot slid out from under me, and I fell to the ground with a squishy thump. *"Eeew!"* I shivered, scrambling up from the slime as fast as I could.

"Look, maybe J.C. was crazy enough to go in there, but I don't think we should," George cautioned.

I gazed up at the building, rubbing my hands

against my jeans to get the mud off. "It looks solid enough," I murmured. But when I grabbed the railing, the whole porch shifted with a creaky groan that made me jump back.

"We'd better not risk it. If the house collapses, I definitely don't want to be inside," I said, making my way back across the mud to George. "But . . . we're so close! How are we going to find out what J.C. was up to?"

"Remember how mildewed Bernard Tilden's journal was?" George said thoughtfully. "I'll bet you anything that it was right here in this house."

Her theory made sense. And my gut told me that J.C. was the one who found the journal and returned here last night looking for more. So why was Craig standing next to the journal when I found it?" I wondered out loud. "We were pretty sure he dropped it. Unless . . ."

As I thought back, the picture of Craig staring down the street at the glowing taillights of a car flashed in my mind. "Right before I found the journal, Craig was watching someone drive away," I told George. "What if *that* person dropped the journal, not Craig?"

"J.C. did tell Deirdre he had to leave early," George said. "And I don't remember seeing him when we were dancing after you found the journal."

"Still, all we have is guesswork," I said, scraping my boot across the mud-coated pavement. "There's got to be a way to prove J.C. is the one looking for the money. I mean, if he took those framed photos, he must have them somewhere. . . ."

"His hotel?" George suggested. "Didn't Travis say the guys on the team are staying at the River Heights Motor Lodge?"

"Yes, he did." I started back down the muddy road toward my car. "J.C.'s probably at the foundry," I said, "so let's start with the hotel."

George and I were both relieved to leave the flooded part of Cedar Plains behind us—and to make it past the barrier without any police spotting us. Before long we were pulling up in front of the River Heights Motor Lodge. The U-shaped building was two stories high, with doorways on both levels and stairs going up to a second-floor balcony. At the center of the U was a swimming pool surrounded by lounge chairs. It wasn't warm enough to swim yet, and the pool was empty except for a layer of grime and leaves.

The place was quiet—and the more deserted the better, as far as I was concerned. We didn't exactly want an audience while we snuck into J.C.'s room.

"There's the reception desk," George said, nodding at a glassed-in office at the end of the U-shaped building. "Let's find out what room J.C. is in."

As we got out of the car, I scanned the first- and second-floor doorways. Three laundry carts stood on the walkways outside the rooms, along with buckets, mops, and bottles of cleansers. As I watched, a woman wearing a white smock over her clothes came out of one of the second-floor rooms. In her arms was a mound of towels and sheets, which she dumped into her cart.

"I'm not sure reception will be so accommodating—but maybe there's a better way," I said. "Come on."

We jogged up the stairs and caught up to the woman as she was opening the door to the next room. "Excuse me, miss," I said breathlessly.

"Yes?" The woman turned toward us, and I saw that she had chin-length black hair and small wrinkles at the corners of her eyes and mouth. "Can I help you?"

"We hope so," George said. "We're trying to find J.C. Valdez. He's one of the basketball players who's staying here."

"You mean the Bullets? Such lovely boys!" the woman said, her voice filled with warmth. "I call them my knights in shining armor. Every day I thank those boys for helping to build the apartments over at the Davis Foundry. See, my three boys and I lost our place down in Cedar Plains during the floods and—"

"You're going to get one of the foundry apartments when they're done?" George guessed.

The woman nodded. "Let me tell you, it'll be a relief when we don't have to sleep on the floor at my sister-in-law's place anymore," she said. "She's been a darling to us, but after a while you just want your own place, know what I mean?"

"Mmm," George said. "Did you say you *do* know which room is J.C.'s?" she pressed.

"Sure, I know. Room 226. It's right down there," the woman said, nodding farther down the second-floor balcony. She reached for a bottle of spray cleanser with one hand and her keys with the other.

"Do you think you could let us in?" I asked before she could disappear into the next room. Seeing her hesitate, I added quickly, "There's something in there that's desperately needed at the foundry. Work could be held up if we don't get it soon."

It wasn't a *total* lie. Work *would* be held up if there was any more damage to the foundry. Still, I wasn't sure the woman bought our story. For a moment she just stood there sorting through her keys. But at last she smiled and said, "Well, I guess it's all right. . . ." Stepping farther down the balcony, she unlocked room 226 and pushed the door open. "Just close up when you leave. The door will lock automatically."

And just like that, we were inside.

"Yes!" George whispered. "So, what are we looking for?"

I heard the cleaning woman's footsteps fade away as I took a quick glance around the room. It was a pretty standard motel layout—bed, TV, desk, closet, minifridge, and bathroom. I headed to the desk first and began opening drawers.

"We're looking for the framed photos that were taken, for one thing," I told George. "Or anything else that connects J.C. to the damage at the foundry. A sledgehammer, silver spray paint . . ."

As George slid open the closet door, I bent to look underneath J.C.'s bed. As soon as I lifted the hem of the bedspread, a sour, moldy smell hit my nose.

"Either the River Heights Motor Lodge needs to do a better cleaning job, or something that's been in the floods is under here," I murmured.

Pressing the side of my head against the carpet, I spotted some boxlike silhouettes under the bed. I reached for the closest one and pulled out something smooth and wooden.

"It's one of the missing pictures from the foundry!" I exclaimed. Reaching back underneath the bed, I quickly pulled out two more. "Yup. Here's the old building plan and those photos we saw our first day at the foundry, of people working there back in the nineteen fifties."

"So J.C. *did* steal them!" George said breathlessly. "And that's not all. Look at these, Nancy!"

I glanced up to see her step away from the closet with a handful of clothes that definitely belonged in the laundry carts outside. In one hand were a pair of jeans and a polo shirt so muddied that we could barely make out the blue color underneath the grime. Hanging from the other hand was a pair of sneakers caked with a familiar, sour-smelling slime.

"He's definitely been nosing around where the floods were," George said. "Or tromping through the muddy bank under the window of the foundry, where we saw footprints."

"There's something else under here too," I added. Putting my head to the floor, I reached for the last remaining object under the bed. I nearly gagged when my fingers touched slimy wood. "Ugh!" I said. Still, I made myself hold on to the moldy-smelling thing. I pulled it out into the light, then sat back on my heels to look at it.

"It's an old cigar box," I said. "A fancy one, from Cuba."

George dumped J.C.'s muddy clothes to the floor and bent over the box. "Didn't Bernard Tilden write in his journal that he stole Cuban cigars from Mr. Davis?" she asked.

"Mmm. So maybe this is the box they came in, huh?" I said. The box was still damp and was coated with the same moldy slime as J.C.'s clothes. Touching just a corner of the wood, I lifted the lid.

"Oh my gosh!" George said. "We hit the jackpot, Nancy."

That was for sure. I lifted out a gleaming gold pocket watch and fingered the initials that were etched into the gold cover. "KD," I said. "Kenneth Davis, the owner of the Davis Foundry. . . . This is the watch Bernard Tilden stole from him!"

I grimaced at a handful of soggy, awful-smelling cigars that filled one side of the box. But the other side, where the watch had been, was filled with old newspaper articles. They were yellowed and damp. But I managed to peel the top article free and spread it out on the carpet.

"It's from the *River Heights Bugle* on May thirtieth, nineteen fifty-five," George said, looking down at the weathered newsprint. She pointed at the headline: THIEF GETS AWAY WITH GOLD.

I had already skimmed the first paragraph, describing the theft of Kenneth Davis's gold watch by an "unknown intruder." Leaving the clipping on the carpet, I reached carefully for the next one: UNEXPLAINED

THEFTS CONTINUE AT DAVIS FOUNDRY. "This one talks about the stolen cigars and company seal," I said.

"You mean this?" George leaned over to pick up a heavy metal seal from inside the moldy cigar box. She fingered the raised lettering on the seal. "It's got a picture of the building with the words 'Davis Foundry, Incorporated' around it in a circle."

"Remember how smug Bernard Tilden sounded in his journal?" I said. "He was definitely proud of getting revenge without Mr. Davis having a clue to what he was up to. I bet Tilden cut out these articles himself as a kind of proof of how clever he was."

"What a jerk," George said, shaking her head in disgust. "Is there anything in there that tells where he hid the money?"

I turned back to the box, but—except for the soggy cigars and clippings—we had emptied it.

"What about this?" I said, pulling the framed floor plan of the Davis Foundry closer. That was when I realized that the glass had been removed and that someone had made marks on the plan. "Hey, it looks like J.C. wrote on this."

George pointed to two circles that had been inked over the plan. "Aren't those the two hidden rooms that were uncovered?" she asked.

"Yeah. But he's written some question marks, too,"

I said. "They're all near where the old offices were. Remember what Tilden wrote in his journal, about hiding the money right under Mr. Davis's nose?"

George nodded. "Looks like J.C. is still trying to find the hiding place, huh?" she said.

I looked from one scrawled question mark to another. One marked a storage closet. Another marked an employee changing room. A third marked the mail room. "None of these look like a place that would be secret enough to stash a half million dollars in," I said. "Unless . . ."

"Unless what, Nancy?" George asked, sitting on the edge of J.C.'s bed.

"Well," I said, staring at the floor plan, "Mr. Eldridge told me the layout of the foundry was altered a few times over the years to suit the company's changing needs. This plan is pretty old. . . ."

"From nineteen twenty-seven." George pointed at the date written at the bottom of the plan, then shrugged. "So?"

"Well . . . what if there are other floor plans showing changes made *after* nineteen twenty-seven?" I suggested. Grabbing the framed floor plan, I jumped to my feet. "Come on. We need to make another visit to the Historical Society."

•   •   •

"I give up," George said an hour and a half later. "I've stared at these building plans for so long, I'm starting to go blind!"

Luther Eldridge had found four different plans to the Davis Foundry besides the one from 1927. Two of the plans were spread out on his desk, and the other two were on the table near the window. We had already gone over three of them, comparing them to the plan with J.C.'s question marks on it. We had found one more hidden space, where an old stack had been walled off when it was replaced with a steel blast furnace. But the old stack was clear across the foundry from Mr. Davis's office—not exactly right under his nose. So George and I had kept on searching.

"Okay, this is the last one. It's from nineteen forty," I said.

My eyes gravitated to the part of the plan that showed the center of the foundry, where Mr. Davis's second-floor office overlooked the main casting shop below. "Hmm," I said, looking back and forth between the new plan and the one with J.C.'s marks on it. "Hey, check it out! The new plan shows a slightly bigger casting shop, but the storage closet from the old plan isn't here at all!" I pointed to the spot on the yellowed plan. "See where Mr. Davis's office is?"

"Right above it!" George said, sucking in her

breath. "You think part of the old closet got walled off when they expanded the casting shop?"

"Could be," I said. Taking a pen from Luther's desk, I circled the question mark J.C. had made next to the storage closet on the floor plan he'd stolen. "One thing's for sure. If there *is* a secret space there, it's right under Mr. Davis's nose . . . just like Tilden wrote in his diary."

George straightened up away from the table, letting out a whistle. "Shouldn't we tell Owen about this?"

"Definitely." I glanced at my watch. "Wow. It's already after five. The Helping Homes teams have probably quit for the day. Especially if the Bullets are going to have another practice session with Brad's team tonight."

Taking my cell phone from my bag, I dialed Owen's number—then groaned when I heard the recorded message for his voice mail. It seemed like forever before the beep sounded and I could leave a message. "It's Nancy, Owen," I said. "Please call me. It's important."

All of a sudden my whole body buzzed with a sense of urgency. "We can't just sit around waiting for him to call," I said. "We need to try to find that secret room—and the stolen money—before J.C. does!"

As we raced out of the office, I saw Luther Eldridge

playing backgammon with Mr. Fillmore at one of the long library tables. "Find what you were looking for?" Luther asked, glancing up from the board.

"I think so. Thanks, Mr. Eldridge!" I called, waving the copy of the floor plan we'd found in J.C.'s motel room.

"Oh—and, Mr. Fillmore?" George said over her shoulder. "I'm pretty sure Brad will be here with good news about Otis soon."

Luther and the white-haired man both opened their mouths, but George and I didn't have time to stop and explain. We were out the door before they could get out a single word. In no time we were back in my car and heading toward River Street.

"Slow down, Nancy!" George said. She shot a sideways glance at me as we screeched around a curve in the road. "Relax. I mean, J.C. can't be up to anything now. He has a practice session with Brad's team, remember? Besides, it's not like J.C. can just waltz into the foundry and bust up more walls—not with a guard on duty at the foundry."

She was right, but somehow, I still couldn't relax. "Half a million dollars is a lot of money. Who knows how far J.C. will go to get it?" I said.

As soon as we came out of the trees next to the foundry, my eyes shot to the one car that was parked there.

"Looks like the guard is the only one here," I said, pulling up next to the police car.

All my senses were on red alert. I was hyperaware of the crashing sounds of the river, the slanting rays of the setting sun on the rocky cliffs, and the crinkling paper of the floor plan in my hand. As we jogged toward the entrance to the foundry, I scanned the building's outside perimeter and the darkening shadows of the building materials under the blue tarp.

"The guard must be inside," I said. I pulled on one of the double doors, and as it opened, I called softly, "Hello?"

George and I stood there in the lobby, listening. When there was no answer, I called again, in a louder voice this time. "Hello! Officer Brandt?"

"He probably can't hear us if he's off in some corner making rounds of the apartments," George said with a shrug. "There's a lot of ground to cover in this place."

I was already stepping farther into the foundry. As I looked around, I saw that the Helping Homes work teams had accomplished a lot that afternoon. The new walls of the lobby had been covered with Sheetrock and taped and plastered, so they were smooth. Glancing up, I saw that the railing of the second-floor balcony had been put up. I didn't see any sign of foul play—at least, not yet.

The part of the exposed brick wall where J.C. had

smashed through was just out of sight—I couldn't see whether it had been repaired yet. But, looking at my copy of the floor plan, I gauged where Mr. Davis's office had been. "Mr. Davis's office was up there," I said, pointing to the brick at the far end of the balcony.

"It looks like the old casting room runs from here halfway down that hallway," George said. She nodded down the corridor that disappeared out of sight to the left of the new lobby. "The storage room that was partly walled off must be behind the walls of the apartment that's just below Mr. Davis's office, right?"

I nodded and checked the floor plan again. "The second one down the hall," I said. "Let's go!"

Shoving the floor plan into my bag, we headed for the hall. As soon as we turned in at the second doorway, I got a prickly feeling at the back of my neck. "Uh-oh," I murmured as my boots scraped against brick dust.

The entryway in front of us opened onto a spacious living room that stretched back to an exposed brick wall. I groaned when I saw the hole that had been smashed through the bricks—and all the reddish brown rubble covering the living room floor.

"Oh my gosh," George whispered. But instead of heading into the living room, she leaped toward the kitchenette that angled off the foyer. When I followed, I saw Officer Brandt sitting on the floor with his back against the kitchen wall. His wrists and ankles were bound with wires, and a bandanna was tied over his mouth as a gag.

"Officer Brandt! Are you all right?" I asked, bending down next to him.

Officer Brandt grunted, his eyes shifting wildly.

"What is it?" George asked, tugging at the bandanna over his mouth.

The officer strained against his binds more urgently. As soon as George pulled the gag free of his mouth, he rasped out, "Behind you!"

Even as George and I whirled around, I heard scraping footsteps on the floor behind us. J.C. Valdez was just climbing into the living room through the hole in the bricks. I gasped when I saw the huge sledgehammer he held. He swung it ominously back and forth as he walked toward us.

"Make a single move," he said, "and I'll kill you."

15

Thief's Reward

George and I froze, our eyes on the heavy hammer that swung back and forth, back and forth. Finally, I gulped and shifted my gaze to J.C.

"Congratulations," I told him. "Looks like you found the forgotten room Bernard Tilden wrote about in his journal."

"You got *that* right," J.C. gloated. Then he frowned slightly. "What do *you* know about the journal?" he asked.

"You dropped it at Deirdre's party, and Nancy found it. We know all about the money Bernard Tilden stole from Mr. Davis," George said. Her eyes kept flicking curiously toward the hole in the bricks. "So . . . is the money in there? Did you find it?"

J.C. didn't answer right away but just kept his sledgehammer swinging. At last he gestured toward the hole and said, "See for yourself. Both of you. I want you where I can keep my eye on you."

Uh-oh, I thought, looking around. Not that there was anyone nearby who could help us. "What are you going to do to us?" I asked.

"You'll see." J.C. jerked his head toward the hole a second time. "Now quit stalling and get in there."

George climbed through the ragged hole first. I squeezed through after her, into a triangular room barely large enough for the two of us. At our feet a wooden crate sat among the dust balls, spiderwebs, and pulverized brick. The crate had obviously been sitting there for ages. A lacy network of dusty cobwebs covered the outside of it—and the cracked wooden lid that had been tossed aside. Even in the dim light that came through the hole in the bricks, I saw piles of money stacked right up to the top of the box and several wads that had spilled over onto the floor.

"Whoa! Nancy, we can't just let J.C. take all this money," George said. "It's stolen!"

"Well, who's going to stop me?" J.C. scoffed, leaning into the hole from the living room. "Not you two, that's for sure. In fact, you'll be helping me—if you know what's good for you. Start putting the cash in here," he ordered.

He handed a yellow Bullets sports bag through the opening. George looked questioningly at me as she reached over and took the bag. *What are we going to do?* she mouthed silently.

That same question had been churning in my mind. All I could do was shrug as I reached for a wad of bills and put them in the sports bag. Then my shoulder bag shifted, banging against my ribs, and I felt something hard inside. My cell phone! I thought.

I glanced over my shoulder at J.C. His face was framed by the ragged opening in the bricks, but his eyes were focused on the money, not me. Reaching into my bag, I opened my phone and pressed the button to dial the last number called. George took one look at my hand, deep inside my bag, and began to bang the wooden box noisily against the concrete.

Excellent! I thought. J.C. would never hear my phone with all that noise. Glancing inside my bag, I saw that the call was being answered. Owen had picked up!

"Hey, cut it out!" J.C. said angrily. "Just put the money in the bag."

"Oh, sure thing. Sorry about that," George told him. She stopped banging the crate, but I noticed the tiny smile that curled the outside edges of her mouth.

"How did you sneak back into the foundry, J.C.?" I asked, loud enough so that I was pretty sure Owen would be able to hear me on his phone. "We didn't see your car in the parking lot."

J.C. laughed and said. "Well, I didn't want to take any chances, not after you followed my car up here the other night. I left with everyone else when Owen called it quits for the day. Of course, I drove back up a few minutes later, but I parked behind some trees off the side of the road so the guard wouldn't get suspicious."

J.C. let out another self-satisfied laugh as he added, "The stupid idiot never even saw me coming. I knocked him out from behind and tied him up before he came to."

Glancing into my bag, I saw that the call was still connected. I just hoped Owen could hear what we were saying and guess what was going on!

"Jeez, you're worse than Bernard Tilden!" George said, shaking her head in disgust. "He acted like he was the biggest brain to hit the planet in a century too. But he was just a low-down thief!"

"He deserved that money!" J.C. said hotly. "Everyone in my family knew how badly Mr. Davis treated him."

I shivered when I saw the angry gleam in his eyes. Who knew how long it would be until Owen got here—if he got here. Somehow, George and I had to buy some time—or at least keep J.C. talking. Then I realized what he had just said, and remembered how we'd originally assumed the Bernard Tilden house belonged to J.C.'s parents.

"So Tilden was a relative of yours?" I asked. I had already guessed the answer, but I definitely wanted to keep J.C. talking.

He shot a surprised glance at me. "He was my mother's great-uncle," he admitted. "His house passed to my mom after he died. Too bad no one thought to look in his journal before I . . ." He hesitated, but I had a pretty good idea of what he'd been about to say.

"Before you went in after the floods?" I guessed. "Brad and Tanya said they saw you there. Is that when you found his journal?"

"Police weren't letting anyone in the houses, but I promised my folks I'd get their things. You know, pictures and sentimental stuff," J.C. explained. "Yeah, I found the journal. I guess after Uncle Bernard died so suddenly, the family just shoved it away without reading it. But *I* read it. Good thing I did too. Otherwise, I'd never have known he hid that money here in the factory."

J.C. leaned into the hole, his eyes still fixed on the crate of bills. "It figured that Helping Homes would pick the exact same time to fix up this place into new apartments. Volunteering on the job was the only way I could look for the money."

"Let me get this straight," George said, standing upright in the tiny space. "You didn't volunteer with Helping Homes in order to help people. You did it just to get the money? And in the meantime, you didn't care if you *hurt* all the work we were doing?"

J.C. just shrugged. "I knew it might take some time to find the money, since my uncle didn't write exactly where he hid it. That was why I went back to the house last night, to see if maybe he left anything *else* saying where the money was."

"Why did you try to pin the damage on Craig Reynolds?" I asked J.C.

"It was too perfect," he said, with a smug laugh. "I mean, after I took that floor plan, I needed a way to distract people's attention from me. And Craig had already knocked me down, so people knew how he felt about me. When I stashed the frames in my car, I saw a box full of spray paint in his truck bed. The rest was easy."

"Your phony accusations could have ruined Craig's life! Did you ever think about that?" George asked, grabbing more cash and putting it in J.C.'s sports bag.

J.C. just shrugged again.

I kept glancing past him, watching and listening for some sign of help. Where was Owen? Somehow, George and I had to buy more time. "What happened at Deirdre's party, J.C.?" I asked. "Someone was in the garden with me. I thought it was Craig, but . . ."

"It wasn't easy to get rid of Deirdre, but when I saw you and your friends go outside, I figured you might be talking about the foundry," he said. "I snuck outside and listened. Too bad Craig decided to get curious about what *I* was up to. I barely got away without him seeing me."

But I saw *him*, I realized. "You must have dropped Bernard Tilden's journal before you drove away."

"None of that matters now," J.C. said. He scowled into the darkening shadows at us. "All that matters is that I've found the money. A half million dollars . . ."

"You won't get away with it," George said hotly. "The police will know you took it."

"Not if you're not around to tell them," J.C. told us. There was a steely edge to his voice that chilled me to the bone.

"What are you going to do to us?" I asked.

His eyes shifted to the handle of the sledgehammer.

"Never mind about that. Just hurry up," he said.

There were just a few more wads of bills left in the wooden crate. George reluctantly grabbed them and placed them in the sports bag.

"Hand it over," J.C. instructed.

As he held out his hand, I saw a flash of movement behind him. Owen? I didn't want my eyes to tip off J.C. Lowering my gaze to the bag, I picked it up slowly. "Oops!" I said, pretending to stumble.

J.C. scowled as money spilled out across the floor. "Cut the shenanigans," he said sharply. He gripped the sledgehammer, but before he could lift it, I heard a loud thud.

J.C. slipped to the floor, out cold.

"Nancy! George!" Owen said, appearing on the other side of the hole. In his hand was a chunk of brick. "Are you okay?"

George and I grinned at each other. "We are now," I told him. "We're fine."

"Smile and say cheese, everyone!" said Owen, a week later.

Bess, George, Tanya, and I squeezed in next to the other Helping Homes volunteers in the lobby of the Davis Foundry. "Cheese!" we all said. There was a flash of light as the photographer for the *River*

Heights Bugle snapped off a shot. In the next instant the volunteers let out a wild cheer and green Helping Homes caps flew up into the air like confetti.

"Congratulations! We did it!" Owen cried above the din, ducking caps that rained down on us. "The foundry is now officially open and ready for residents."

The cheering grew even louder. I spotted Brad and Cathy farther back in the crowd. If their wide smiles were any indication of how they felt, they were definitely happy.

"Talk about a dramatic makeover," George said as we headed for the tables where punch and cake were being served. "It's only been a week and a half, and the foundry is ready to move into."

"Can you believe it?" Bess glanced around at the shiny silver elevators and freshly painted walls and balcony. "The elevators are in, the bathrooms have been tiled, all the cabinets, sinks, tubs, and toilets are in place, and pipes and wires are in working order. Whoever would have thought that a bunch of regular people like us—with a little professional help—could pull off such a big job in such a short amount of time?"

"Or that we'd have to catch a thief while we were at it," Tanya added. She raised an eyebrow at me, shaking her head. "What a shock for everyone to find out their favorite basketball star was the person who was wrecking all our work."

"Well, at least J.C. is in jail now," I said. "And we still managed to finish renovating the foundry right on schedule."

"I'll toast to that," Craig Reynolds spoke up next to us. He and Cam had just helped themselves to glasses of punch, which they raised. Craig put his arm around his brother's shoulder. "And even though J.C. Valdez proved himself to be the jerk I thought he was all along, not *all* of the Bullets are bad news."

Cam gazed over his shoulder at Travis and some of the other guys wearing yellow Bullets warm-up jackets. "We learned a ton from training with the team—even without J.C. Coach Stanislaus thinks we've got a good shot at being number one in our league next year."

I turned to see Owen working his way through the crowd toward us. "Helping Homes should have a great season too," he said. "A great building season, that is. I just heard from the lawyer for the Davis family—"

"The ones who owned the foundry?" Bess asked.

Owen nodded. "They never expected to get back the money that Bernard Tilden stole from them all those years ago," he said. "They decided the best way to use the money would be to donate it to the *next* Helping Homes renovation for flood victims in the area."

"That's great!" I told him.

I picked up a glass of punch, but it spilled a moment later when someone bumped into me from behind.

"Make room, people," Deirdre Shannon called out. She had the *Bugle* photographer by the arm, and she pulled him over to Owen. "I'm sure readers will want to see a picture of me with Mr. Parkinson."

"That's *Jurgensen*," Owen said dryly.

Deirdre gave a dismissive wave of her perfectly manicured hand. "Whatever," she said. "The point is, I threw a fabulous party, and I *am* Helping Homes' biggest fan."

"Really?" George asked, raising an eyebrow. "Does that mean you'll be volunteering for the next renovation?"

"You mean . . . working?" Deirdre said, her smile faltering.

Owen nodded. "Helping Homes could use all the help we can get," he told her. Then he turned to Bess, George, Tanya, and me. "What about you four? Can I count on you for our next project?"

I hesitated for half a second. Just that morning I'd

gotten a phone call. I couldn't give my friends any of the details—not yet, anyway. But it looked like I would be heading to California for a few days.

"When would we start?" I asked Owen.

"Let's see . . . It'll take a week or two to get all the paperwork done. But we'll start as soon as possible after that," Owen said. He gazed at me with eyes that sparkled with challenge. "What do you say, Nancy? Think you can handle it?"

"Are you kidding?" Bess said, grinning. "Nancy Drew is *always* up for another adventure."

"True," I agreed. "Absolutely, most definitely true."

REDISCOVER THE CLASSIC MYSTERIES OF NANCY DREW

THE HARDY BOYS

UNDERCOVER BROTHERS™

They've got motorcycles,
their cases are ripped from the headlines,
and they work for ATAC:
American Teens Against Crime.

CRIMINALS, BEWARE:

THE HARDY BOYS ARE
ON YOUR TRAIL!

Frank and Joe tell all-new stories of crime,

danger, death-defying stunts, mystery, and teamwork.

Ready? Set? Fire it up!